PRAIRIE
WIDOW

PRAIRIE
WIDOW

HAROLD BAKST

M. EVANS
Lanham • Boulder • New York • Toronto • Plymouth, UK

Published by M. Evans
An imprint of Rowman & Littlefield
4501 Forbes Boulevard, Suite 200, Lanham, Maryland 20706
www.rowman.com

10 Thornbury Road, Plymouth PL6 7PP, United Kingdom

Distributed by National Book Network

British Library Cataloguing in Publication Information Available

Library of Congress Cataloging-in-Publication Data

The hardback edition of this book was previously cataloged by the Library of
Congress as follows:

Bakst, Harold.
    Prairie widow / Harold Bakst.
      p. cm. — (An Evans novel of the West)
    I. Title. II. Series.
    PS3552.A4384P73   1992
    813'.54—dc20
    92-5292

ISBN: 978-1-59077-332-1 (pbk. : alk. paper)
ISBN: 978-1-59077-333-8 (electronic)

∞™ The paper used in this publication meets the minimum requirements of
American National Standard for Information Sciences—Permanence of
Paper for Printed Library Materials, ANSI/NISO Z39.48-1992.

Printed in the United States of America

Chapter One
Under a Kansas Sky

Perched next to her husband on the seat of their covered wagon, and with a pot of sickly purple geraniums on her lap, Jennifer Vandermeer at last saw on the treeless horizon a cluster of buildings, all sitting as if in a vice between the tawny-green prairie and the lowering dark sky.

"Ha!" blurted her husband, a big, ruddy-faced man sporting a wide-brimmed hat. "There it is!" He turned to his wife, but her dour profile quickly subdued his enthusiasm. He returned his attention to the distant town and gave the reins a flick.

His four oxen, however, unimpressed, continued in their slow, plodding way, their heads down and bobbing as they went, their yoke chains gently rattling.

It would take a while for the wagon to cross the great intervening distance, and Jennifer found herself once more lulled by the heat of the early summer day, the monotony of the endless, sweeping grasslands, and the creaking of the wagon's axle. When, finally, the town was close enough to see it better, Jennifer sat forward, her curiosity piqued. But she was quickly disappointed: the buildings had false facades, like so many theater sets, fronting what were really weather-worn hovels. Some were made of prairie marble—bricks of sod. There weren't even any boardwalks, but only loose planks laid down on the dirt along the front of the buildings. Four Corners' foothold on the prairie seemed all too unconvincing. The sea of thigh-high grasses crowded the buildings, coming right up to the sills of the outward facing windows and infiltrating down the two prairie paths that intersected the town's center.

"Peter! Emma! Wake up!" called Jennifer's husband, leaning back and turning his head toward the interior of the covered wagon. In a moment, two sleepy faces appeared. The boy, around eleven years old, had his father's blonde hair and blue eyes; and the girl, a couple of years younger than her brother, had her mother's delicate build and dark hair. "Is this Four Corners?" asked the boy.

"It must be," answered the father, growing excited again. The wagon approached the first outlying building, which had big open doors, and a furnace and anvil inside. A slender man with thick forearms and a leather apron stepped outside. Jennifer's husband pulled on the reins, and the oxen stopped. "This Four Corners?" he asked.

"You found it," said the man, his face glistening with sweat. He approached the wagon and stopped by a rear ox, patting its rump.

"My name's Walter Vandermeer," said Jennifer's husband. "This is my wife, Jenny, and my two children, Peter and Emma."

"Pleased to meet you," said the slender man. "Name's Frank Turner. Where you from?"

"Ohio."

"Ah. I'm from Indiana myself. Been here five years now." Frank Turner looked at Jennifer. "Welcome ma'am."

But Jennifer smiled only faintly and averted her eyes.

"My wife's kind of tired," explained Walter quickly.

"Sure. It's a God-awful journey. I don't know how the

women do it. Anyway, your timing's not bad.'' He gestured with his head toward the dark sky.

''Yeah,'' agreed Walter, ''it looks like it's going to come down hard.''

''Then don't let me keep you. You're probably looking for the land office.''

''That I am.''

Wiping his neck with a handkerchief, Frank Turner pointed toward the center of the cluster of buildings. ''That's it, next to the general store. The agent's name is Bill Wilkes.''

Walter craned his neck and squinted in the general direction.

'' He's not been too popular around here lately,'' continued the blacksmith, tucking his handkerchief into a back pocket. ''But that's what happens when you get more than two people together—politics.''

''I guess so,'' said Walter, flicking the reins. ''Thanks for your help.''

Frank Turner patted the ox on the rump and backed up. ''You'll need that axle greased,'' he called.

Walter directed his wagon into the center of town and pulled up in front of a small, sod-brick building with a wooden awning. The sign read:

U.S Government Land Office
Bill Wilkes, agent

There weren't many people on either of the two intersecting streets, but those who were there nodded a greeting and waved. Walter returned a smile, even as he muttered to his wife, ''You can at least try to be friendly. They're going to be your new neighbors.''

But the very suggestion made Jennifer stiffen, and she lifted her chin defiantly.

Shaking his head, Walter lowered himself to the ground.

He stretched. "Peter, Emma, close up the wagon," he said as he went up to the front of the oxen and began tying the lead pair to a crooked cottonwood limb that served as a hitching post. "Then come inside. It's going to rain." He looked to his wife. "Jenny, you're welcome to come in, too."

Jennifer turned her head away. She found herself looking across the dirt street at a building that also had a wooden awning, whose support post had a sign reading, Pearson's Inn.

"Suit yourself," said her husband as her children began excitedly drawing in the canvass around the opening at both ends of the wagon.

Walter was in the land office only a moment before he reemerged. "He's not in there. I'll check the general store." He paused a second and eyed his wife. "Jenny, don't be so stubborn. When the children are done, come in with them." But, again, Jennifer didn't answer. Grumbling to himself, Walter disappeared into the neighboring building, which had a sign over its door, Franz Hoffmann's General Store. Between the two buildings was narrow alleyway that revealed a slit of the surrounding prairie.

"We're done, Momma. Are you coming in?" asked Peter, standing on the ground near the wagon seat.

"No, you and your sister go ahead," said Jennifer quietly.

"But it's going to rain," insisted Emma.

"I'll be fine. You go join your father."

Her two children walked the few steps along the planking and entered the general store.

The sky, meanwhile, was getting very dark. Other people began making their way to the store. But Jennifer, resting the geranium pot next to her, sat primly in her seat, her hands now folded in her lap.

A moment later, Peter stepped outside and called, "Momma, Poppa said not to be stubborn and to come inside."

"Tell Poppa I'm quite content to remain here."

Peter went back in. Jennifer peered up. A pale-bellied bird streaked across the dark sky, just high enough to clear the false facades.

Then Jennifer heard a faint thump on the wagon's canvass. She thought it might have been another bird. Then she heard a clack just in front of the land office, and she saw what appeared to be a smooth, white pebble roll off the plank and into the dirt, where it began to melt. This was followed by a second clack, as another white pebble bounced off the wagon's tongue between the two oxen. Now the clacking and thudding began to grow in rapidity and in volume as ever more white pebbles dropped from the sky, bouncing and rolling across the wooden awnings, wagons, and the two dirt streets. The oxen began to get jittery as an occasional pebble smacked their hides. Pretty soon, Jennifer, shielding her flowers, was herself struck smartly on the shoulder. She hurried off the wagon with her pot, nearly tripping over the hem of her long skirt. The pebbles fell in full fury just as she hurried into the general store.

"Damn, hailstones in July," said one man over the thudding on the roof. He was standing before the window and gazing out. Across the rump of his pants was a patch stamped with the words, "ava Coffee," the "J" being missing from "Java."

"This is going to knock the hell out of the wheat," commented an older, square-built man with short, white hair. He stood by a makeshift bar, which consisted of two barrels, upon which rested a short length of hickory board. On a shelf behind the bar was a single bottle of schnapps.

"Ach, dis iz zomet'ing, all right," added a tall man wearing an apron, standing behind the main counter. His slick, dark hair was parted in the middle, and his face was red, as if from too much schnapps. He cleaned a ceramic stein with a rag as he spoke.

Jennifer, remaining near the open door, quickly scanned the rest of the room, which was jam-packed with what seemed to be every conceivable type of merchandise. Several barrels were scattered throughout, one filled with pickles, one with crackers, another with nails. Some hard salamis hung over the counter, which itself held a large, round cheese and a glass jar of white-and-green peppermint sticks. Behind the counter and the red-faced man hung a cuckoo clock, its hands and weights still. Nearby were shelves holding dishes with brightly colored scenes painted in their centers. There were drinking glasses of all heights, tea cups and saucers, beer steins, general bric-a-brac, and, leaning in one corner, several blank headstones.

"I hope Todd had sense enough to take in the laundry," remarked one woman to another, both of whom were standing by an unlit stove in the middle of the room. The first woman held by her side a little barefoot boy, roughly Peter's age, who was sucking a peppermint stick. The boy and Peter kept eyeing each other from a distance.

"So you decided to join us," called out Walter to Jennifer. His hat off, he was standing by a barrel with another man, who boasted a healthy set of muttonchops and, hanging from his hip, a gun. Emma was there, too, clinging to her Poppa. Jennifer approached. "This is Mr. Wilkes, Jenny," said Walter, unburdening his wife of her flower pot. "He's the land agent."

"Ma'am," said the bewhiskered man.

Jennifer nodded coolly.

"Mr. Wilkes will be showing us our land," said Walter.

"As soon as the hail stops," said Wilkes. "It won't last long." He looked across the crowded room and out the window where the man with the patched pants was standing. The hailstones were already slowing down. The thudding on the roof became less intense.

"I don't know that I've ever seen hailstones in summer,"

commented Jennifer quietly. "And such large ones."

"Why, this is nothing," said Wilkes. "I've seen hailstones as big as my fist!" He made a fist and showed it to Jennifer— "Yep, one thing I've learned since coming out here is there's no telling what'll fall out of a Kansas sky." Wilkes called across the room, "Say, Seth, remember sixty-six?"

The man by the window turned, the coffee label on his rump disappearing. But he didn't answer Wilkes. Indeed, he seemed only to scowl at him. Then he turned to look out the window again.

Wilkes seemed unaffected by this treatment. "He lost all his crops that year," he explained quietly. "Had to find work in the next county."

"But why—" started Jennifer.

"Grasshoppers," said Wilkes. "They came out of nowhere, just like the plague in the Bible—covered everything—crawled into people's houses, got into their clothing . . ."

Jennifer closed her eyes as if to block out the image.

"It'll be frogs next, I suppose . . ."

"Ah, Mr. Wilkes," interrupted Walter, noting his wife's paling complexion, "perhaps we can set out now."

"Sure, be glad to," said Wilkes. "Didn't mean to upset anyone."

Walter replaced his hat on his head. Still holding Jennifer's pot, he took Emma's hand with his free one and called Peter, who had slowly inched his way nearer the barefoot boy with the peppermint stick.

Following her husband, Jennifer was stopped by the boy's mother. She was a dark, slight woman, no more than five feet tall, with black hair and intense, dark grey eyes. "Mrs. Vandermeer," she said, "I'm Lucy Baker, and this is Nancy Camp." She gestured to the other woman, who was tall, and whose fairer skin was sunburnt—"It seems we will be neighbors."

Jennifer marked the two women's worn faces, their faded calico dresses, and she could do no more than hurry on. Outside, the sky had risen, and streaks of blue were appearing. The two streets were already turning muddy from the hailstones melting in the summer heat, and the planks squished beneath Jennifer's shoes.

"Settle down," murmured Walter to the oxen, all four of which were jittery from the pelting. He patted their broad, heavy heads, one by one. He placed the flower pot back on the wagon seat.

"I'll get my horse," said Wilkes, heading off toward the blacksmith shop.

Walter continued stroking one of the oxen. "Peter, Emma, open the wagon."

Jennifer, meanwhile, stood patiently on a plank, her hands clasped before her.

"Jenny," said Walter quietly, still petting the ox, "if you don't start acting friendly, you're going to make us outcasts before we even settle in."

"Hm!" grunted Jennifer, looking off in another direction.

Walter took a long, exasperated breath just as Wilkes rode up on a bay horse.

"Tie your horse to the back of the wagon," suggested Walter, stepping up to meet him. "You'll ride up front with me."

"Don't want to crowd the missus off the seat," said Wilkes.

"That's quite all right," said Jennifer, "I'll sit inside with the children and let you two men talk."

And so, while the two men talked up front, Jennifer sat in her rocker, which didn't rock because it was tied with heavy cord to a plow and various furniture. Her pot once more on her lap, she faced backward, gazing out the back of the wagon at Wilkes's trailing bay while the axle creaked beneath the floorboards and a gentle, warm breeze wafted in through the wide front opening. Peter and Emma sat on the floor at the rear, wedged between a crate and a bureau, taking turns looking through a stereoscope. Jennifer watched the town slide slowly back toward the horizon, sinking ever deeper into the tall grass.

"I imagine you'll want to start planting as soon as possible," said Wilkes to Walter.

"Yeah," answered Walter, "I've got a John Deere breaking plow back there. I'll be planting corn."

"You know, in these parts, the grass is little bluestem," said Wilkes, "and people do better with wheat. If it's corn you want, you should have stayed farther east, where the big bluestem grow."

"The best land's taken back there."

"Not if you look. Why, if I were you, I'd reconsider eastern Kansas. There's more streams back there, better rainfall . . ."

"Maybe so," said Walter, "But I'm here. And here's where I'm planting corn."

Hm! Now who's being stubborn! thought Jennifer.

Four Corners, meanwhile, had dropped from sight. There was little now on the subtly rolling terrain to show the passing of the miles. The very trail—lined here and there with pink-clustered flowers that attracted swarms of monarch butterflies—sometimes grew indistinct, and grasses brushed under the wagon's floorboards.

By and by, the wagon pulled off the trail, continued several dozen yards, then stopped.

"This is it!" announced Walter, "Everyone out!"

The wagon jostled as everyone dropped off—except for Jennifer, who remained stolidly in her rocker. And she stayed like that for several minutes, listening to the muffled voices of her husband and Wilkes, occasionally the voices of her children, and always the gentle blowing of the prairie wind.

Finally, the mutton-chopped visage of Wilkes appeared in the rear opening of the wagon, startling Jennifer.

"Well, I'll be heading back now, Mrs. Vandermeer," he said as he untied his horse's tether from the wagon.

Jennifer forced a decorous nod.

Wilkes leaned toward her. "I can't say I blame you for feeling this way," he said almost in a whisper. "It's pretty rough-going out here."

Jennifer arched an eyebrow.

Wilkes straightened. "Anyway, good luck to you." He tipped his hat and walked over to his horse. Jennifer watched him ride away toward the trail.

Then Walter, his ruddy face even redder than usual, appeared in in the opening. "I hope you're pleased with yourself," he growled. "Now Wilkes is going to have a grand time telling everyone how you acted like a spoiled little girl and refused to come out of the wagon."

"I don't care," said Jennifer quietly.

"You will next time you have to show your face in town."

"I don't plan to."

"Never?"

"Never."

"Oh, you'll have to. Now, why don't you stop making a fool of yourself and get out of the wagon."

"No thank you, I'm comfortable right where I am."

"Damn you!" snapped Walter, stalking off a few feet, then returning to the wagon. "I won't put up with this much longer!"

"Where are the children?"

"They're fine! Now are you coming out of there, or aren't you?"

Jennifer turned her head away, looking over the plow handle at a jumble of chairs. Again Walter stalked off, and Jennifer wondered whether her stubbornness was pushing her husband too far. He returned.

"You know, I really ought to start breaking ground," he complained. "It's late in the season."

"You go right ahead."

"Yeah, but first I've got to get you out of there. Hand me the shovel."

Jennifer furrowed her brow, but she didn't ask why Walter wanted the shovel. She reached behind her, took it, and offered it to him. He grabbed it and stalked off.

Soon, she heard him digging. She was curious, but she dared not look, even though it was getting hot in the wagon.

But then, several minutes after the digging started, Jennifer was jolted from her chair by the shouting of her children. "Poppa! Look out!" cried Peter.

Jennifer put her pot down and stuck her body out the back of the wagon. She saw, some yards off, Walter swinging frantically with his shovel at some squat, furry beast in the grass. "Walter!" she screamed. She scrambled from the wagon and hurried to him, hoisting her skirt to keep herself from tripping.

"Stay back, everyone!" roared Walter, taking a swipe at the grizzle-coated animal, which snarled back and returned the swipe with its own long claws, ripping Walter's pant leg.

Jennifer dashed to her children and yanked them behind her. "My God, Walter, where's your gun?"

His blue eyes bulging, Walter kept swinging his shovel as if he were using a scythe, but the beast kept dodging it, lunging spryly this way and that, slashing back.

"Walter!" cried Jennifer, making a tentative step toward her husband.

"Poppa!" cried the children from behind their mother.

"Keep them back!" shouted Walter as he landed a good whack on the animal's broad back, then another on its side.

The beast, its striped face locked in a snarl, began to back up. Walter didn't follow. When there was some distance between the two combatants, the animal turned and, still growling, waddled off into the grass. Jennifer and her children now hurried to Walter, who let the shovel drop to the ground.

"Are you all right, Poppa?" shouted Peter.

"Walter," cried Jennifer, hurrying to her husband's arms. "Well, look who's out of the wagon," said Walter, his chest heaving, his face sweaty and red.

Jennifer pushed him away at arm's length but kept her hands on his broad shoulders. "Are you hurt? Your pants are ripped."

Walter looked down at his shredded pant leg. "Well, that old badger got the worst of it." Jennifer started to bend to check her husband's leg, but he stepped away and walked over to a small rise in the land, which was taller than he. It was in the side of this rise that he had been digging. He checked along the base and stopped. "Ha!" he shouted, "It looks like I was breaking into a badger den. See the entrance?" He pushed back some grass.

The two children ran over to see.

"Peter! Emma! Be careful!" shouted Jennifer. Keeping her own distance, she craned he neck and looked. "My God, Walter, why were you digging there, anyway?"

"I was preparing our home," he answered. He noted the den. "And now it seems I've been given a head start. I'll just expand this burrow until it's big enough for the four of us and our furniture."

Jennifer felt woozy. "Walter," she began slowly, "surely you're not suggesting that we are going to live inside this hill."

"I surely am, little lady. There are no trees around here for a proper cabin, and this is the quickest way to get us some shelter. Don't worry, you won't be the only one living this way. Remember that stand of wheat we saw with no house around? There was probably a dugout nearby."

Jennifer closed her eyes and stepped back. "Walter, I will not live in a badger hole."

Walter approached his wife. "Listen, Jenny, it won't be a badger hole when I'm through with it. You'll have a door and windows . . ."

"I will not have the children living in there."

"Hell, they'll probably think it's fun—right, children?"

Peter's and Emma's eyes widened with joyous expectation.

"Yay!" shouted Peter.

"Yay!" echoed his little sister.

Walter turned back to his wife. "See?"

"No, Walter," insisted Jennifer, "I'm sorry. I want to go home."

At this, Walter could only clench his teeth and glare at his obstinate wife. He picked up the shovel. "You are home."

Chapter Two
Digging In

Over the course of the next week, Walter kept enlarging the badger den. He made the entrance big enough to allow his own broad physique, and continued hollowing out the inside, eventually poking a square hole on either side of the entrance for windows. At the end of each day, he declared that he was done because the dugout seemed spacious enough—until, that is, he moved in a piece of furniture. Then he realized how small the room still was. So, the following morning, he resumed his digging.

Meanwhile, Jennifer, now that she was out of the wagon, stayed out, if only to tend to her children. Walter had scythed away the grass from a small area where she could cook without setting the prairie on fire. Nearby she set up some chairs, a table, and a packing crate, which served as a kitchen counter. She even set out her rocker so that she could watch Walter digging as she rocked back and forth in grass that came up to her armrests and tickled her forearms. The wagon itself provided her with a semblance of a wall in what was otherwise an endless expanse that reached in every direction to the single encircling horizon. On bright days, Jennifer noted how the wind might continuously comb the grassy sea, and sheets of light would glide across the bent stems like fleets of magic carpets, beckoning her east.

But Jennifer stayed only in her rocker, feeling very small in the midst of all that open wilderness—and positively insignificant beneath its enormous capping blue dome. The prairie sky, she noted, was everywhere you looked. It was above you, it was in front of you. It was in back of you. It was everywhere except beneath you.

But as bad as it was during the day, the prairie during the night was still worse. Once the sun lowered to eye level, smearing the western sky with color and reddening the prairie and broadside of the covered wagon, Jennifer grew frightened. The sky darkened in the east, where the stars first appeared, spreading westward until they were overhead and all around, encrusting the entirety of what was now a black dome. With no moon out, the great grassy expanse disappeared in darkness. Jennifer could no longer see, only listen to what was out there beyond the glow of her campfire. Mostly there was the chirping of insects and the gently blowing wind. Sometimes, there was the chilling, yet poignant, howl chorus of distant wolves. On those occasions, Jennifer didn't sleep. She kept her children close to her inside the wagon, and she didn't relax until the sun returned, appearing at eye level on the opposite horizon, reddening the great grass expanse from that direction.

It was none too soon for Jennifer when Walter finally did dig out enough room in the hill to fit all the furniture and all the family—if just barely. He finished the job by putting in pole rafters—brought from Ohio—to keep the prairie sod above from sagging in. He then installed the cookstove, shoving the stove pipe right through the dirt ceiling and out among the prairie grass above. Finally, with Ohio lumber, he built a proper wooden door and two window frames with shutters. Unfortunately, there were no glass panes to put in those frames.

"Where do you want these chairs?" he asked Jennifer as he began hauling furniture through the doorway. "Where do you want this chest?"

Jennifer didn't answer. She didn't think it much mattered where they were placed in that hole.

"Where should I put this clock, Poppa?" asked Peter, carrying in a mantel clock.

"Where should I put these books?" asked Emma, hurrying with one volume under each arm.

Jennifer stayed back and watched as all her lovely furniture, scratched and dull from the long journey, was now shoved into this cave, in a squat Kansas hillside. Only when her husband and children were done moving in, and the wagon—her only home for hundreds of miles—was stripped of its canvass top, did Jennifer at last go in to inspect her new home, bringing with her the pot of geraniums.

Her heart sank. Though it was pleasantly cool inside, the room was murky, with only a feeble light entering through the two windows and door. And her beloved furniture, placed cheek-by-jowl, appeared merely as poignant momentos of her bygone life in the civilized East. She located her rocker, which Walter had placed near the cookstove, and she brushed from its needlepoint seat some soil that had fallen from the ceiling. Then, while Peter and Emma played outside, and while Walter hitched the oxen to the plow, Jennifer rocked back and forth, the geraniums on her lap once more. The smell of the earthen walls was in her nose, and the room's grave-like silence pressed upon her ears.

Over the next few days, Jennifer went grimly about her wifely duties. One thing she learned quickly: it was going to be impossible to keep her home clean. The loam sprinkled down continuously from the root-laced ceiling. The table, the cookstove, the pots and pans, the silvery daguerrotype of her father, the high-backed chairs, the few books, as well

17

as the hard dirt floor itself, all had to be swept daily.

Then there were the intruders. Ever so often, Jennifer had to pluck an earthworm from the low ceiling, or a mole would push its way through her walls, blindly sniffing the sudden, open area before retreating.

Walter, meanwhile, devoted his attention to matters outside the home. He broke the sod, which peeled back in long strips from his curved, steal plowblade. He cut through the tough mesh of grass roots—the fabric of the prairie—to the rapidfire muffled clicks and snaps, as if an unending string of tiny, buried firecrackers were being set off. After a few days, he built a shelter of poles and hay for the oxen. And, that afternoon, he went to town to refill one of the barrels with water from Frank Turner's well.

But instead of fresh water, Walter returned to the dugout with a dark-haired, bearded man. He told Jennifer the man's name was Mr. Riley, and that he was a water witch.

"We'll soon have our own well," he told his wife while Mr. Riley, all eyes upon him, walked hunched over around the dugout, holding before him the forked ends of a willow branch. His face was in deep concentration as he walked in ever larger circles, moving steadily farther from the dugout across the plowed field. Finally, about a dozen yards from the door, back in the middle of the wild bluestems, his branch began to dip. He walked a bit farther, and the branch pointed straight down. "Here!" he announced, stomping the ground with his foot. "Dig here."

Walter hurried over with his shovel. "You sure?" he asked.

"Sure, I'm sure."

Walter began to dig. Mr. Riley stood back, stroking his beard.

The water, however, was not very near the surface. Walter dug over six feet down and found no water. "You sure there's water here?" he again asked Mr. Riley, who watched the whole time.

"Oh, you've got to dig deeper'n that," answered Mr. Riley. He fetched his horse while Walter dug. "I'll be in and out of town for a few days," he said from atop his horse. "You can pay me when you strike water."

Walter, his head down as he dug, grumbled some acknowledgement, and Mr. Riley rode off.

By the end of the day, Walter had gone down nearly twice his own height, and still there was no water. He began to curse Mr. Riley under his breath, calling him a charlatan taking advantage of desperate homesteaders. "He won't get a penny."

Jennifer looked smug, which didn't escape Walter's notice when he came up to rest. "You'd better pray we find water," he said, "I mean, it's not as if we're leaving."

This sobered Jennifer, and she began looking anxiously down the hole.

The next morning, Walter had a little trouble finding the hole in the tall grass. When he did find it, he tied a piece of red cloth to the nearby grass, then lowered himself down and resumed his digging. By morning's end, he had gone down nearly the length of his height again. Jennifer by now had to help by hauling up dirt in a bucket. Still, there was no water. Walter dragged himself out as he cursed Mr. Riley and threatened to toss him down the hole and cover him over.

Jennifer almost felt sorry for her husband. After all, he was trying so very hard. Still, he had brought this upon himself.

The next morning, however, when Walter returned to the hole, he found the bottom was muddy. With great excitement, he resumed his labor. Each time Jennifer hauled up the bucket, she found the mud was looser and looser. Soon, it was muddy water. Then the muddy water became clearer. Finally, Walter called up, "Tastes terrific!" When he came to the surface, his pants were wet up to his thighs.

19

That night, Walter wished to celebrate. And he knew how he wanted to do it. It was two weeks since he and Jennifer moved into their new home, and longer than that since they had been intimate. There had been no privacy on the westward journey, and, as far as Jennifer was concerned, there still wasn't. She and Walter shared just the one room with their children.

But Walter would not be put off any longer. The dugout, after all, was pitch black at night, and the children slept on the opposite side of the room. So, as soon as the children's gentle breathing showed that they were asleep, and with a warm breeze blowing in through the two windows, Walter pressed close to his wife, his hand sliding under her nightgown, across her belly, his lips nuzzling the curve of her neck. Jennifer resisted at first, but, really, she wanted to be close, too. When Walter finally slid on top of her, slowly hoisting her nightclothes above her thighs, she whispered in his ear only, "Don't make noise."

After that night, life in their new home was little less tense. It was with some amazement that Jennifer one day realized that she had been living on that Kansas prairie for one month. She had never imagined herself surviving so long in such a God-forsaken place. The heat at times could be brutal. And she couldn't escape it on that treeless land except by retreating into her dugout. And while she hadn't noticed many mosquitoes when she first arrived, there were soon plenty of them to add to her misery.

Then there was the wind. It didn't seem to ever stop blowing. Unhampered by anything vertical within view, the wind sometimes whispered, sometimes groaned, sometimes screamed. But always it was there, and it threatened to drive Jennifer mad.

And, yet, it didn't. Jennifer simply went about her duties:

hauling water from the well, bathing her children, washing clothes before her door on the scrubboard, sewing buttons, plucking earthworms from the ceiling, sweeping the dugout, and stoking her cookstove with, of all things, buffalo chips.

But whatever the inconveniences and hardships she had to endure, she discovered that there was one burden that proved to be the very worst—one, indeed, that only weighed more heavily on her with each passing day—the loneliness.

In all that time and, despite all the immensity of land contained within her view, she saw—aside from her own family—not another human being. In the evening there was no light from any distant window. During the day, there was no smoke from another stovepipe. No wagons passed on the trail.

Jennifer fondly remembered how she used to be able to sit on her front porch back in Ohio and, raising her voice only slightly, speak to the neighbors on their porches; or how, on summer evenings, she would greet neighbors, dressed in their best clothes, as they strolled by her house down the lane colonnaded with massive tulip trees. "Good evening, Charles, Dorothy," she would say, languidly fanning herself. "Good evening, Jennifer," they would respond, Charles always tipping his hat. "Nice evening." Their four children would hurry ahead. "Isn't it, though?" Jennifer would add, "A little muggy perhaps . . . "

But no neighbors strolled past Jennifer's dugout now. Indeed, it seemed at times that her family was the only one left on the planet.

And so it was with some relief that, one morning, Jennifer finally espied a group of people walking up the trail toward her homestead. One stooped figure was on horseback. Walter was away, which made her nervous, but she saw, even at a distance, that there were at least one woman and two children in the approaching party, and so she didn't worry. Indeed, she ground some coffee, primped in the mirror hanging outside the dugout, and waited outside her door, occupying herself with some darning. She would not be as cold to her neighbors this time as she had been in Franz Hoffmann's store.

It took a long while before the party came close enough for her to make them out better but, when she did, Jennifer's enthusiasm turned to terror, and she looked about to see where her children were. "Peter! Emma! Get inside!"

"What's the matter, Momma?" asked Peter, walking up to her, a tin soldier in his hand.

"Just do as I say," responded Jennifer, ushering him along.

"Look, Momma, people!" announced Emma, pointing as she, too, was swept along by Jennifer into the dugout. Jennifer herself went in and closed the door, which had a latch but no lock.

"Momma, who are those people?" asked Peter, looking out the window.

"Get away from there," snapped Jennifer, tugging him back.

"But who are they?"

Jennifer pulled her children to the deepest recess of the dugout. She stared at the door and two bright windows, which showed within them, like two paintings, the tawny prairie and blue sky. "Shush!" hissed Jennifer. "Stay here."

Jennifer approached the windows. She peered out and gasped. The band of people were walking from the trail toward her dugout. Jennifer spun around to face her children. "Where does Poppa keep his gun?"

"Why do you want that?" asked Peter.

"I'm scared," said Emma, her eyes watering as she stepped away from the dirt wall.

Jennifer pushed her back. "I said stand there." She turned to Peter. "Where's Poppa's gun?"

"I'm scared too, Momma."

"Don't be!" snapped Jennifer as she began frantically searching through the dugout.

"Momma! Look!" squealed Emma.

Jennifer spun and faced the windows. In one was a portrait of a grim, dusky-faced man with long, braided hair. He was dressed in a red blanket, and three feathers were sticking from his head. Without ceremony, the man stepped in through the window, even as the door opened and another man, wearing a red blanket, his long hair unbraided, entered.

"Indians, Momma!" declared Peter.

Jennifer pushed him and Emma behind her skirt, her heart pounding nearly out of her chest. Before her were the first Indians she had ever seen outside a book. "God, please protect my children," she whispered.

The two men looked about the furnished cave, the first one picking up a pewter mug and inspecting it, the other, his face pock-marked, apparently from a bout of smallpox, studying the picture of Jennifer's father. Then the first man, putting down the mug, returned his attention to Jennifer. He pointed outside the door to an old man on a sorrel pony, two little boys, and a woman carrying a papoose across her back. He gestured as if shoveling food into his mouth. Jennifer hurried to get them some food. The first man then said something to those outside, and they came in, crowding the little dugout.

While Jennifer prepared to serve them some flapjacks, bacon, and corn dodgers, the Indians walked about the gloomy room, squeezing themselves among the furniture. The man with the pock-marked face flipped blankly through the pages of the King James Bible, pausing to look at the engravings. The young woman with the papoose investigated first the mantel clock sitting on the bureau, putting it to her ear, and then she opened the drawers and pulled out one of Jennifer's undergarments, rubbing it against her cheek. The two boys, roughly Emma's age, picked up Peter's tin soldiers from the dirt floor while Peter watched nervously. The old man, toothless, his face weathered and cracked, approached Peter and stroked the boy's long, blonde hair, which unnerved Jennifer, and she hurried even faster to set the food on the table.

When she did set it out, the Indians pulled up chairs and packing crates to sit on, and they began to eat with their fingers. They said nothing, and Jennifer said nothing either, but just stood as if in waiting, her children behind her. Whenever one of the Indians finished what was given to him, he lifted his empty plate and gave it to Jennifer, whereupon she quickly refilled it. Even the old man and the young woman had huge appetites, for they kept asking for more, always more.

Jennifer was certain that when the food ran out, the Indians would turn on her and her children, butchering them all. Surely Peter's blonde hair would make a particularly good trophy for their tepee. Or maybe they were all to be kidnapped—her children to be raised as savages, herself to become the white concubine of an Indian brute.

The Indians were still eating, exchanging an occasional word among themselves in their own language, when Jennifer heard Walter's wagon approaching.

"Poppa!" cried Emma, hurrying to the window.

The first two Indian men jumped to their feet. The one who had come in through the window returned to it and looked out, standing behind Emma.

Tears bursting from her eyes, Jennifer pushed her way in front of the man and cried out what she thought were her final words, "Walter! Go back! Indians!" And, with that, she slumped to the floor, grabbing Emma and holding her to her heaving breast.

Walter froze. He peered at his dugout and the sorrel pony tethered to a post out front. The man wearing the feathers stepped out the door, followed by the pock-marked one, who was, in turn, followed by the others.

"Good woman," called the first Indian.

Walter descended from the wagon and hurried past the Indians, who opened a path for him to his door. Inside, he found Jennifer crumpled on the floor, sobbing with Emma. Peter was standing near them, also crying.

"Jenny! What happened?" asked Walter, crouching next to his wife and cupping his hand on her head. Behind him, the Indians crowded the doorway and watched.

Jennifer lifted her head and peered up with reddened, watery eyes. She embraced her husband around the neck with one arm while still clinging to Emma with her other. "Indians, Walter! They just came right in!"

Walter turned and looked up at the Indians. The feathered one appeared puzzled. "Good woman," he repeated with emphasis.

Walter took a deep breath and rose. He faced the Indian. He raised his chin to look bold but furrowed his brow to look sincere. "Forgive my wife," he said, "I think she lost her mind."

All the rest of that afternoon, to Jennifer's horror, Walter entertained his Indian guests. After they finished eating, he offered them some of his tobacco, and they in turn offered him some of theirs. Walter kept trying to engage them in conversation, but they didn't understand English. Still, he wouldn't give up. "What tribe?" he'd ask, using his hands as if they might clarify what he was saying. "Where from?"

The Indians' response was either just a smile, a nod, or some words Walter himself couldn't understand, even when the Indians added some supposedly clarifying hand gestures of their own. So mostly everyone sat silently, except for an occasional word exchanged among the Indians themselves. The woman with the papoose sat in Jennifer's rocker, the two boys kept eyeing Peter's tin soldiers, much to Peter's annoyance, and ever so often one or another of the men would add a respectful nod in Walter's direction.

When the visit was finally over, and the Indians filed out of the dugout, Jennifer quickly closed the door. Walter, still puffing on a pipe with tobacco the Indians had given him, looked sternly at Jennifer. "You gave me quite a scare earlier, yelling out the window that way."

Jennifer reddened.

"I thought I told you the Indians around these parts aren't violent."

"Perhaps you did—only how could you be sure?"

"I ought to be mad with you," said Walter, releasing a puff of smoke, "but I'm not."

"Hm! You probably think I'm a fool."

"No, you thought I was walking into trouble. It's like when you came running during my scrap with the badger. I guess that means, even after all I've put you through, you still kind of like me."

Jennifer was reluctant to answer at first. "I'm used to you," she said.

"Yeah, well, I'm more than used to you. Come here." Jennifer begrudgingly approached, and Walter embraced her. "I'm sorry, Jenny. About all of this. But don't you see, it's the only chance I've got to make something of myself. We couldn't stay in your father's house forever."

"I was happy there."

"I know. Maybe I did a mean thing dragging you out here. If it helps any, I think about that a lot. And I feel bad about it."

"But you insist we stay."

"Damn it, we've got to."

"You mean you've got to. This is for yourself. You're not thinking of me or the children."

At this, Walter's face turned dark. He released Jennifer and backed away. "That's not fair. I'm making a life for all of us out here. You'll see." And with that, he left the dugout.

26

Jennifer was left standing there, wondering if she had said too much. She hoped that she hadn't ruined his mood for the rest of the evening. When Walter returned, half an hour later, she greeted him with, "Dinner will be ready in a bit," but, as it turned out, it was now Walter's turn to be the silent one.

"Is Poppa angry?" asked Peter, sitting with Emma at the table.

"He's tired," said Jennifer, flipping some corncakes in a pan. Then, wiping her hands on her apron, she went to Walter and said softly, "You're upsetting the children."

Walter, sitting on a packing crate near a window and puffing on his pipe, glared up at her. "You're a fine one to talk," he growled. But then he eyed Peter. His face relaxed. "Hey, son," he called, "why look so gloomy?"

Peter approached his father tentatively. "Are you mad?"

"Nooo, like Momma said, I'm just tired. In fact . . ." Walter rose and knocked the ash from his pipe onto the window sill. "I think I'll go to bed."

Jennifer raised her eyebrows and glanced at the clock on the bureau. "Why, it's not even seven o'clock. You haven't eaten."

"Yeah, well, I really am tired," responded Walter, shuffling over to the bed. He didn't even bother taking off his clothes. He just threw himself down and lay on his back, breathing through his mouth.

Jennifer stepped up to him. His face was glistening slightly from perspiration. "You look pale," she said.

"Do I?" he asked, his eyes shut.

Jennifer reached over and put her hand on his forehead. Walter opened his eyes, but said nothing. He waited for the diagnosis.

"I declare," said Jennifer, removing her hand and standing straight, "I do believe you've come down with a fever."

Chapter Three
The Shakes

Walter was the stubborn one. Jennifer knew it. But it was never more clear than the next morning. Though he awoke achy and wet with perspiration, he insisted that he go into the field to break more land.

"Walter, you will stay in bed," said Jennifer quietly so as not to awaken the children.

But Walter only smiled warmly at his wife's concern, and he pulled on his denims.

"I mean it," continued Jennifer. "It's crazy to work in your condition."

"And if I don't go out there, who will?" asked Walter, pulling on his shoes. "You? Peter?"

"Surely you can wait a day."

"A day? I could be laid up all week. No, I've got work to do." Walter rose and slipped on his shirt, even as he convulsed with a shiver.

Jennifer, her hands on her hips, glared at her husband. He put his hands on her shoulders and gently shunted her aside so that he could step away from the bed. He lifted his wide-brimmed hat from a crate and put it on. "Don't worry, I'll sweat the fever out."

"This is sheer madness . . ."

Walter opened the door, about to step out into the cool,

blue air of dawn. Already several birds were singing in the air, where, in a normal place, there would have been tree branches. Before leaving, Walter turned and faced his wife. "Look, I know what I've got to do. I told you last night that I mean to build us a life out here, but I can't do it by lying in bed."

"If you're doing this to prove something . . ."

"I'm doing this because I have to. Prairie folk don't make excuses. Our neighbors are made of stern stuff. I won't do less than they."

Walter seemed so intense about it that Jennifer couldn't offer another word to counter him. She just watched as he headed for the ox stalls.

For the rest of that morning, Jennifer went about her chores, first preparing bacon and eggs for the children then, while they ate, sweeping out the dugout. Every so often, she glanced out the windows or the open door to see how Walter was holding up. Each time he was hard at work behind the four oxen and plow some dozen yards from the door, slicing away at the sea of grass, which hid him from the waist down. In his wake, blackbirds gathered to feed on the insects that clung to the exposed underside of the turned sod. Every so often, the blackbirds were scared into flight as a kestrel dove down to snatch up a field mouse or snake, whose tunnel or burrow had been torn open.

Then something odd happened.

Jennifer had been watching Walter through a window while she gathered the breakfast dishes, and she averted her eyes for only a moment. When she next looked out, Walter was gone. The oxen were still there, still and legless in the tall grass. But Walter had vanished. Jennifer stepped outside. "Walter!" she called. There was no answer. "What on earth?" She scanned the field. "Walter!"

Jennifer walked first slowly toward the plow, then more quickly. When she got close enough, she finally saw Walter lying face up on his plowed black furrow. "God! Walter!" She dashed to his side and dropped to her knees. "I knew it, I knew it!" she whimpered. "Peter! Come help me with Poppa!" She pulled Walter's arm around her neck.

Peter and Emma came running. "What happened?" shouted Peter.

"Poppa isn't feeling well. Put his other arm around your shoulder."

Peter did this, and both mother and son helped Walter out of the grass and back into the dugout while Emma followed, carrying her Poppa's hat.

When she got her husband to bed, Jennifer returned outside to unhitch one of the oxen from the plow. "Now, you watch Poppa while I'm gone," she said to her children as she led the ox to the wagon. "Make sure there's water in the bucket next to his bed and, if he needs help drinking, tend to him."

"Yes, Momma," said Peter. "Where are you going?"

"Into town to get a doctor." Jennifer hauled a harness from the wagon and began hitching the ox, her dark hair falling in ringlets across her forehead, moist with perspiration.

"Are you leaving us alone?" asked Peter.

Jennifer crouched and put both hands on Peter's shoulders. She looked him squarely in the eye. "You are to watch after your sister, as well," she said. "Do you understand?"

"Yes, Momma."

"Stay with her in the house. Neither of you are to go outside for any reason. Stay close to Poppa."

"Yes, Momma."

Jennifer rose and finished hitching the ox. She pulled herself onto the seat. "Now go inside."

Peter took his little sister by the hand and led her into the dugout. He closed the door. Jennifer flicked the reins, and the ox pulled the wagon toward the trail.

When she arrived in Four Corners, Jennifer rode straight to Frank Turner's blacksmith shop. Frank came out of the big double doors, wiping his neck with a red handkerchief. "Well, Mrs. Vandermeer, I haven't seen you since you arrived," he said. "How's the homestead?"

"Walter is ill," said Jennifer bluntly. "Is there a doctor in the area?"

"Oh, I'm sorry to hear it. Anything serious?"

"He has a fever. Please, is there a doctor?"

Frank Turner grimaced at having to disappoint Jennifer. "The closest we have to a doctor is Lucy Baker. She's pretty good fixing people up."

Jennifer recalled the name. Lucy Baker was the small, dark-eyed woman who had introduced herself in Franz Hoffman's store. Jennifer had been cold to her and her friend.

"Her place is west of here." Frank Turner pointed down one of the two prairie paths that intersected the town. "Go out that way and her soddy will be on your right. You can't miss it. You'll see it from way off."

Jennifer thanked the blacksmith and directed her ox through town and out the other side. She rode onto prairie that was especially flat, and the trail, bordered here and there with those pink flowers attended by monarch butterflies, was more deeply rutted than the one that led to her homestead.

Later, Jennifer saw a soddy some distance off. She rode and soon noticed that the wild bluestems to her right were replaced by wheat. The soddy was now not far off, and Jennifer roused herself.

Frank Turner had used the term "soddy," and not "dugout." And it was true that on land as flat as the Baker's homestead there was no rise in which to gouge out a shelter. So, instead, they built their house with that prairie marble: blocks of sod cut out from an acre of ground and stacked like bricks into foot-thick walls. Supported on poles and brush, the sod even served as a roof, from which grass still sprouted. Jennifer had seen several such soddies on her westward journey. There were crude looking, but not as crude as a dugout, and the Bakers had morning glory vines gracing their door. Also, rather impressively, an elm grew next to their soddy—the only tree within the entire horizon. Indeed, it was the only one Jennifer had seen since her family's wagon had crossed a stream in eastern Kansas, where cottonwoods and willows had lined the banks. The stream was cut so low in the ground that only the tops of the trees peeked out, at first looking from a distance like mere bushes. At the sight of the elm, Jennifer's heart lifted, even if the tree did look a little bedraggled from the constant wind. Like the vines, it was no doubt planted by the Bakers, perhaps brought from the East as a sapling.

There were a few smaller buildings near the soddy, some also made of sod bricks, others like the chicken coop and cow stall, of poles and hay. Jennifer heard several voices coming from behind one of the sod buildings, and then she saw a naked little girl, about five years old, step around the corner. She stood by the building, her thumb in her mouth, staring with big, dark eyes at Jennifer. She was soon followed by a small, wiry woman, Lucy Baker, who was holding a blanket. "Mary!" she called. "Don't go wandering off!"

Jennifer braced herself. She hoped that her neighbor didn't remember the snub. "Good morning," she said.

Lucy Baker, wrapping her child in the blanket, looked up. "Oh, Mrs. Vandermeer. How are you?"

"I'm fine . . ."

Just then, a stoop-shouldered teenaged boy, himself wrapped only in a blanket, stepped out from behind the building. "Come on, Maw, are my clothes ready?" But the boy, noting the lady visitor, quickly retreated back behind the building.

"You've caught me on a wash day," explained Lucy. She sent the little girl back with a pat on her rump. "Tell your Paw we have company."

"Please," said Jennifer, "I can't stay. I was told that you do some doctoring."

Lucy stepped up to the wagon, her dark eyes serious. "Is someone sick?"

"My husband. He's got a fever."

Lucy Baker turned grim. Without another word, she went into her soddy. Jennifer, still sitting on her wagon seat, wondered what to think. Then Lucy's husband came out from behind the building, tucking his shirt into his pants. "Morning, Mrs. Vandermeer."

Jennifer remembered him, too, from Franz Hoffmann's store. He was the man with the coffee-label patch. Jennifer had thought it rather unfriendly, the way he responded to Bill Wilkes, but he certainly didn't seem unfriendly now. Though his clothes were a bit frayed, he was still an amiable enough looking man, even handsome, with black hair, pale grey eyes, and an apparently steady smile.

Lucy Baker, wearing a red sunbonnet and armed with a satchel, reemerged. "Walter Vandermeer is sick," she told her husband as she hauled herself up onto Jennifer's wagon.

"Bad?" asked her husband.

"He fainted in the field," said Jennifer.

"Tell Todd to fetch Nancy and to bring her to Mrs. Vandermeer's house," said Lucy to her husband. "Come, Mrs. Vandermeer."

Jennifer flicked the reins, and the ox began to plod.

"You needn't go back through the town first," said Lucy. "Just cut across that way." She pointed in a direction off the trail and straight across the sea of grass.

Jennifer did as her neighbor instructed, and the ox pressed into the long stems, the wheels of the wagon turning in the grass like the paddle wheels of a Mississippi riverboat.

Along the way Lucy asked Jennifer about Walter's symptoms. Jennifer told Lucy what she could, and then, for a while, the two women didn't talk. Finally, Jennifer said, "I'm

34

sorry I was so rude to you in Mr. Hoffmann's store.''

"Oh, that's quite all right," said Lucy. "You're not the first unhappy wife to be dragged out this way by her husband. It must be pretty awful for you."

"Yes. Awful."

"You'll get used to it."

"No," said Jennifer, shaking her head, "somehow I don't think I will."

Lucy checked in her satchel—"Where are you from?"

"Ohio."

Lucy closed her bag. "We passed through Ohio on our way out here. We're from Pennsylvania. Here eight years. Left home right after Seth got back from the War."

"Eight years! Tell me, did you mind much when your husband took you out here?"

"Mind?" Lucy Baker raised her eyebrows. "Heavens, no. It was my idea."

By and by, the wagon broke onto the faint trail leading to Jennifer's homestead. Again, the two women didn't say much more until Jennifer spotted her dugout in the shallow rise. "There," she said with some embarrassment. "That's where I live."

Soon, she pulled the wagon up in front of her dugout, and Peter opened the door and stepped out.

"How's Poppa?" asked Jennifer, afraid of the answer.

"He doesn't talk," said Peter, looking very worried. "He just lies there and shivers."

Lucy Baker lowered herself to the ground, took her satchel from the seat, and marched in. Jennifer followed.

Inside the somber room, Walter lay on his back trembling and sweating profusely. Emma stood by the bed, holding her ceramic-faced doll and watching her Poppa. Lucy approached, removing her bonnet and pulling a high-backed chair with her.

"Are you a doctor?" asked Emma.

"I'll have to do" Lucy reached over and put a hand on Walter's forehead.

"How does he look?" asked Jennifer.

"Like he's come down with the shakes," said Lucy, opening her satchel. "Heat some water, will you?"

"The shakes," repeated Jennifer softly as she went to do Lucy's bidding. For the rest of the day, she continued to do whatever Lucy instructed. But mostly, she watched as her neighbor administered to Walter bitter quinine and ginger tea doped with extra vinegar, smeared his chest with plaster of turpentine and lard, bathed his feet in a hot bath, and kept him generally wrapped up to his neck in a blanket. When Nancy Camp arrived, dropped off by Todd Baker, she took over the assisting, and so Jennifer watched from farther off.

"Is Poppa dying?" asked Peter, standing near her.

The thought clutched Jennifer, but she said, "No, of course not. Come on, let's all go out for a while." And she took Peter and Emma outside.

It was now late afternoon, and the sun was low in the clear blue dome. Emma sat herself on some trampled grass before the dugout with a miniature setting of chairs, table and tea service. She bid Peter to join her and Melissa, her ceramic-faced doll.

Peter, however, didn't want to. He stayed by the dugout door and slumped to the ground, absent-mindedly poking at his shoes with a long grass stem.

Jennifer stood by the door as well, clasping her elbows close to her. But she didn't want her children to see how upset she was getting, so she started to wander off, circling to the rear of the dugout, which meant climbing up the rise. When she reached the top, standing now a few feet from the projecting stove pipe she saw, stretched before her, high ground upon which grew shorter grasses. The tips didn't even reach her knees. Jennifer gazed out across this expanse, dotted here and there by the occasional yellow daisy, and she listened to the somber wind.

She stepped forward, scaring into flight a large grasshopper, which resettled on a stem farther off. Jennifer sighed. Could this really be happening to her? Was she really here? It all seemed like such madness. Only desperate people would come to a place like Kansas. Was it really so bad back home?She continued to walk, the short grasses sweeping her skirt. A mourning dove suddenly broke from cover and flew off aways to drop back down out of sight. Jennifer began to formulate a letter she would send her father. She would describe everything about Kansas. He would then certainly insist she come home. And, if not that, then he would at least be sorry he let his son-in-law take his daughter away. Jennifer would derive some satisfaction in that.

She walked on. She now noticed, a dozen paces ahead, an owl standing on a dirt mound. It was a funny little bird with relatively long legs that no doubt allowed it to see over the grass. The owl looked straight back at Jennifer with amazed, slightly annoyed orange eyes. The two stared at each other for several moments. Jennifer stepped closer, and the owl began bobbing up and down. Jennifer paused, enjoying the comical display. She then resumed walking towards the bird, which, seemingly exasperated, dropped down a hole in the mound. Jennifer stopped. What a strange way for a bird to flee! She considered investigating the hole, but remembered her ailing husband and decided to go back.

When she turned, however, a panic rose in her, for she saw no sign of her homestead. Only open grassland. The pipe had vanished.

Jennifer stood there, scanning the distance, unsure which way to go. Each direction looked the same. Surely, though, if a silly owl could find its hole in all this grass, she could find hers. "Now think," she whispered. "The sun was in front of you when you walked away from the stove pipe, so now I must keep it behind me." Jennifer began to walk, keeping the sun to her back or, rather, her elongated shadow before her.

But she proceeded farther than she thought she had come, and the panic returned. She was tempted to call out for help, but what a fool her neighbors would think her then.

Still, let them think it. It was better than remaining out there when the sun set. In the dark she would never find her way home. And then the wolves would come . . .

Before she could yell however, she saw, several yards to her left, as if rising out of the very ground, Nancy Camp, who was climbing up the rise. "Thank God," murmured Jennifer, and she hurried over to her neighbor. When she got closer, she once more saw the dark stove pipe. "My husband, is he . . . "

"He's asleep," said Nancy. "I'm afraid we must wait a little longer."

For a moment, the two women stood side by side, silently watching the setting sun. Nancy Camp was slightly taller than Jennifer and not, so thought Jennifer, a particularly pretty woman. Her face was long, her hair, parted in the middle and drawn tightly back, was a brown, mousy color, and her skin, like almost everyone's out there, was weathered—indeed hers seemed to have particularly suffered, since she was of a naturally delicate complexion and better suited for bosky regions.

"I must thank you for coming to my place like this," said Jennifer. "I don't know what I would have done otherwise."

"Oh, it's Lucy, really," said Nancy. "I'm just an extra pair of hands for her."

"Still, it was nice of you to come."

Nancy nodded graciously. "You're quite welcome."

The two women stood quietly once more, watching the western sky turn a pastel pink. Then Jenifer had to ask, "How long have you lived out here?"

"Six years. I'm from Maryland."

"Do you miss it?"

Nancy seemed reluctant to answer. "Very much."

"So I'm not the only one."

Nancy seemed hesitant to continue, but then she did. "I often dream I'm back there on our little, no-account farm." She grew wistful.

"Then it was your husband's idea to come out here?"

"I'd like to blame him. But, at the time, I thought it was a wonderful idea."

"And now?"

"Now I'm not so sure."

The two women grew reflective. Streaks of red appeared in the sky as the sun began to sink in the distant grass.

"Kansas is a strange place," said Jennifer.

"It struck me that way, too, when I arrived."

"I just saw an owl," continued Jennifer, growing excited at having found a sympathetic ear. "When I approached it, it didn't fly away like a normal bird, but dropped down a hole."

"Yes, that's the way it is out here. With no trees or rocks, creatures tend to hug the ground, or go below it."

"Like some people."

"You know," said Nancy, also apparently appreciating a sympathetic ear, "even after all these years, I find it unnerving at times—like right now—to be the tallest object around."

"Yes, yes, I know what you mean," said Jennifer. "I feel so—exposed."

"Now, what this prairie needs is a nice, tall church spire!"

"We had a lovely one back home. I used to be able to see it poking up among the tree tops from my upstairs window."

"Are you a churchgoer?"

Jennifer hesitated. "Not the most conscientious, I'm afraid."

"Well, my husband, Will, and I read from the Bible each Sunday. You and your family are welcome to join us."

"Thank you, I'll—keep that in mind."

"Folks live so far from each other, it's hard to gather for any purpose. It's not natural."

"I quite agree."

"At least you have two lovely children to keep you company when your husband is out. Will and I haven't been so lucky, and now that I'm nearing forty, well . . . "

Jennifer was surprised. Her neighbor looked more like fifty. "Tell me, Mrs. Camp . . . "

"Nancy, please."

" . . . Nancy. Have you ever considered going home? To the East, I mean."

Nancy stiffened, and Jennifer felt as if she had transgressed. "Yes, I have," admitted Nancy. "Many times. Will has, too. We've discussed it."

"But you're still here. Six years, you say."

"Well, it's not as if we're certain we want to go back. There's nothing there for us, after all. Meanwhile, the years just seem to fly by."

Jennifer felt sorry for her neighbor. But she was also determined that the same thing not happen to her. Six years is a long time to be in a place like Kansas.

"Well," said Nancy, turning, "I guess we ought to go back in."

"Yes, I shouldn't be standing out here like this. Incidentally, it will be getting dark soon. Perhaps you and Lucy could stay the night."

"Thank you. I think that's Lucy's intention," said Nancy, stepping awkwardly back down the rise. "She never leaves a patient until she's done."

Back in the dugout, Lucy Baker had lit some coal oil lamps. She sat by Walter's bedside, wiping his forehead with a rag.

Jennifer approached and stood there looking at her sleeping husband. "I can take over for a while," she said to Lucy.

Lucy looked up, rose, and handed the rag to Jennifer. "Nancy and I will prepare dinner for us all tonight."

For the next hour, Jennifer sat by her husband, wiping his brow and tightening the blanket, which kept loosening due to his shakes. "Oh, Walter," she peeped, "don't you wish you were home now?"

Later, Lucy called everyone to the table. "I'm afraid we must stretch the food," she said. "You're low on many things."

"We were visited by Indians," explained Jennifer, taking her seat. "I had to keep feeding them."

"Yes, they come to my door, too," said Lucy. "They're from the Osage tribe. It's sad how they go begging."

"Sad, nothing! They let themselves right in. I thought I was doomed."

"That's just the Indian way. They don't have the same sense of property as White people. You could just as readily make yourself at home in their tent."

"I'd hardly do that!"

"Anyway, they're harmless. Believe me, there used to be a lot more of them when we arrived. The government had originally set aside Kansas for the Indians after they had been pushed out of other areas."

"Hm! Then by all rights, we shouldn't even be here," said Jennifer.

"But then it was discovered you could actually raise crops out here, and the Indians were sent packing to reservations in the Oklahoma territory. I imagine if someone finds out Oklahoma is good for something, the government will send the Indians elsewhere."

After dinner, with Peter and Emma amusing themselves in the corner with their toys, the three women arranged themselves in a circle, sitting on the high-backed chairs. Lucy

41

had removed some knitting from her satchel. She began to knit energetically while Jennifer and Nancy sipped ginger tea. The three chatted, telling each other about their homes back east. A tear came to Jennifer's eye when she spoke, and Nancy, likewise, seemed saddened when it was her turn. Only Lucy seemed to have no regrets about leaving the east.

By and by, everyone grew sleepy and went to bed. Jennifer slept near her husband. Lucy and Nancy slept on the children's mattress. And the children slept on thick blankets laid out on the dirt floor. As Jennifer gazed up into the blackness, she found herself strangely lulled by the constant shivering of her husband, and she fell asleep.

The next morning, Walter was paler and weaker than ever. It frightened Jennifer when she saw his face. Lucy also noticed, and she shooed Jennifer away so that she could resume her doctoring.

When Nancy Camp saw Walter, she went to a corner, faced it, clasped a Bible she had brought, and she looked toward the pole rafters. "Lord, God..." she began to whisper.

Jennifer couldn't stand what was happening. She burst from her dugout. She ran to the well, whose sides were built up of prairie sod, and there she collapsed near the bucket and began to sob. Then she, too, began to whisper, "Please, God . . . "

But when Jennifer next looked toward the dugout, she saw, through tear-filled eyes, the somber figure of Lucy Baker standing within the doorway.

"No, no. Go back in," choked Jennifer.

But Lucy did not go back in. Followed closely by a sniffling Nancy Camp, who held her Bible in one hand and a handkerchief in the other, Lucy proceeded solemnly toward Jennifer.

Chapter Four
Bridal Greetings

There was no preacher in Four Corners, so Seth Baker, at his wife's behest, improvised the words over Walter Vandermeer's grave, "Father, who art in heaven, um, hallowed be thy name, accept unto your bosom our friend, Walter Vandermeer..."

Twenty or so neighbors had come to the burial on Grave's Hill, which was really nothing more than a slight rise in the land, and they clustered in a spot freshly scythed around the rectangular pit. They listened patiently to Seth's words, which were competing with a warm, gentle wind.

"Walter had not been among us long before he was taken away, but, ah, he was a good man..."

Though they hadn't known Walter very well, a few of the women were crying. Some of the younger children hung restlessly onto their mothers, while a couple of men anxiously rotated their broad-brimmed hats in their hands or bit their lips nervously, anxious to get back to their fields. Nancy Camp stood alongside her husband, a tall, wiry man whose Adam's apple slid up and down as he and his wife read from their Bible, moving their lips silently. Every so often, Nancy dabbed a tear from her cheek with a handkerchief.

Jennifer, meanwhile, in a dark cotton dress, propped herself against the short, upright post that was Lucy Baker, who had also gathered to her side Peter and Emma. Her own three children stood opposite her across the grave.

" . . . We do not always pretend to understand your ways, O Lord, but we accept them as wise."

At one point, above Seth's voice and the wind, could be heard the whistle of a meadowlark, which was perched several yards away on a tilted headstone, seemingly enjoying the warm summer day. Then, in a yellow burst, the bird flew down the little, partly shaven hill and skimmed across the grass tops.

" . . . We beseech you to take kindly to Walter's wife, Jennifer, and his two children, Peter and Emma, and that you, um, show mercy, amen."

And everyone repeated, "Amen."

At that, two neighbors—middle-aged brothers who shared a homestead—stepped forward and began to shovel dirt into the hole, covering Walter Vandermeer, who was wrapped in canvass only, wood being too scarce and too precious to use for coffins. Behind the two brothers, waiting to be put in place, lay a headstone from Franz Hoffmann's store, its inscription facing the sky.

Lucy Baker gave Jennifer a stoic hug around the shoulder with one arm.

"I hate to leave him here," said Jennifer weakly. "He ought to be home."

"He is home," assured Lucy. "Look eastward. This ground is one with Ohio."

The other neighbors approached Jennifer, mostly a couple at a time, to say how sorry they were and to hold her hands in theirs. Then, on the way to their wagons, some of them stopped by other graves to pay respects to loved ones, and cut back any grasses that had sprouted around the marker. It was only in this desultory manner that the cemetery was kept up, and there was a corner or two that had been rein-vaded by the prairie grasses, which swallowed up entire headstones.

With most of the neighbors now dispersing back across the prairie, Lucy said to Jennifer, "You come home with Seth and me." She still gripped Jennifer's children, both of whom stared glassy-eyed at the slowly filling hole. "I've already told everyone you'll be there tonight, should they wish to pay their respects."

"Thank you," said Jennifer, watching her children. "But, you know, I think I'd like to be alone—for just a while."

"Of course. But let me take Peter and Emma along with me. You'll join us later."

Lucy began to escort the two away, but Emma stopped and looked back at her mother. She began to cry, and Jennifer dashed over, crouching and drawing Emma close. Peter tried to hold back tears, but then he, too, began to cry, and Jennifer pulled him close so that the three were in each other's arms.

Lucy turned to Seth. "Put ours in the wagon," she said softly. "I'll be with you in a moment."

Seth nodded and herded his own three children into the back of his wagon.

"Shh, shhh," whispered Jennifer in her children's ears.

"I want Poppa," choked Emma.

"I know," said Jennifer.

"I wish we never left home," said Peter.

"But we did," said Jennifer, rising to her feet, angry with Walter again. She pressed her children toward Lucy, who reached out to take them. "Go with Mrs. Baker," said Jennifer.

"Why aren't you coming?" peeped Emma, wiping her tears.

"I will."

Lucy took Peter and Emma to her wagon, and they climbed

onto the back with the Baker children. Then Lucy climbed onto the seat next to her husband. "You remember the way to my place?" called Lucy as Seth flicked the reins, starting up his black mare.

"I remember," answered Jennifer, returning her gaze to her husband's grave. The hole was finally filled, and the headstone was in place. It read:

Here Lies
Walter Vandermeer
Beloved Husband
and Father
at Peace
in God's Embrace
1834-1873

Shovels in hand, the two brothers walked over to Jennifer. "The Lord wanted 'im," was all the older one mumbled, not so much as looking at Jennifer as he walked past. The other seemed to want to offer his own condolences, but he only lowered his eyes and continued on to the buckboard, which was drawn by two mules.

The brothers' wagon was the last to rattle down the shallow hill, and Jennifer was left standing alone among the sprinkling of headstones and mingling grasses. The meadowlark was back and caught Jennifer's attention, perched as it was on a tiny cross, one of two tiny crosses set side-by-side. Jennifer noted the inscriptions. Both were Baker children, neither of whom had survived infancy. Then the meadowlark flitted over to another headstone, this one belonging to a Herman Whittaker. Then the bird flitted to yet another, as if it were showing Jennifer all the people who once lived on this prairie.

"Oh, Walter," whispered Jennifer, barely hearing herself above the wind. "Do you see what you've done? Do you see where you've left your wife and children?" Jennifer dropped to her knees. She brushed her hand over the dark loamy soil that covered her husband. She felt her throat tighten. She didn't care what Lucy said. This was a strange land, and she couldn't bear the thought of leaving Walter buried in it while she and the children returned to her clapboard house and her own Poppa.

Jennifer's eyes glazed over as she wondered what her father, a widower, was doing that very moment. She looked at the sky. The sun was low. It was past the dinner hour, later back in Ohio. Her father was probably sitting in his heavy, cushioned chair and reading the Gazette. It had been his ritual for as long as Jennifer could remember. All through her childhood, each evening, he retired to the parlor and his chair to read while she, his only child, cleared the kitchen table and washed the dishes. Afterward, she would join him in the parlor and listen to him gripe about something in the paper—in those days, the Southern secessionists—while she would sit in her mother's rocker and read a book or do her needlepoint. Sometimes, her father would look up from his paper to comment on something he had just read, and she and he would discuss it though, really, Jennifer mostly listened.

That's the way it had been for so very long, and though she had fancied that she'd like to marry one day—and had spent a good deal of time imagining what the man would be like—Jennifer remained quite content to be the little housewife to her father, even as she turned nineteen, an age when a young lady ought to be married, as, indeed, all her childhood friends were.

But Jennifer's father was not so content. He complained to Jennifer often about her withdrawn ways, and every time he discovered an eligible bachelor—like the coalman or a fellow town clerk—he'd point him out to Jennifer and say, "Now, he would make a fine son-in-law!" But, to his never-ending frustration, either Jennifer proved to be too shy, or the young men had eyes for someone else, someone, perhaps, more fun.

Eventually, Jennifer's father grew so annoyed at his daughter's complacency that he took matters into his own hands. One evening, he arrived home after work with a dinner guest: a big, ruddy-faced man with blonde hair and blue eyes—someone, as Jennifer judged it, about ten years her senior.

"Jenny, I would like you to meet Mr. Walter Vandermeer," her father said, tottering at the doorway, for he almost always made a stop at O'Reilly's Tavern on his way home. " . . . a fine, upstanding citizen, and a Dutchman to boot."

"Miss Schuyler, it is my great pleasure to meet with you," said Walter, himself a mite unsteady on his feet, for it was at O'Reilly's the two men had met. "Your father has told me so much about you."

Jennifer remembered that meeting very well, as if it were much more recent than thirteen years ago. A polite enough evening ensued, but it didn't bode well for serious courting. The two men were clearly more entertained by each other's bawdy company than by anything that Jennifer could contribute.

"And what do you do for a living, Mr. Vandermeer?" she offered from her rocker.

Walter suppressed his high spirits and tried to respond seriously. "Oh, a little of this, a little of that. I'm what you call a Jack-of-all-trades."

"The man is going places!" declared her father, lest there be any doubt.

But there was doubt. Jennifer's first impression of Walter was that he was nothing more than a braggart, a tippler and, worst of all, a ne'er-do-well, something to which her father apparently had decided to turn a blind eye.

Indeed, how angry he used to get with her when she showed no interest in her would-be gentleman friend. "You'd better not be so independent!" he had scolded her on a number of occasions. "Other women—prettier women—have their eyes on him! They know a good man when they see one."

As it happened, though, Jennifer was not quite as independent as her father thought. She had no other man in her life, aside from the grocer, whom, actually, she only spoke to when she went shopping. And she was going to be twenty soon. If the truth were known, she liked it when Walter came calling, as he generally did on Sunday afternoons, equipped with flowers for her and cigars for her father. The two men inevitably shared the cigars, along with some brandy, later in the evening.

By and by, after enough of such Sundays, Jennifer even allowed herself to take a liking to this Mr. Vandermeer. He was, after all, a rather chivalrous sort, cheerful, and a brawny handsome man.

And so, one Sunday afternoon, while her father discreetly excused himself from their company, Walter finally asked for her hand, and Jennifer responded, "Why, that would be very nice. Yes."

And so they were married.

Her father was so happy that he immediately bought Jennifer a slender book entitled *Bridal Greetings*, by the Reverend Daniel Wise in which, as the author wrote, "The mutual duties of husband and wife are familiarly illustrated and enforced." Jennifer was grateful to her father for this gift, for the sweet, little book explained the various problems that couples were subject to in the areas of money, family, friends, the home, and so on, and so forth. She eagerly read a new chapter each night in bed before going to sleep, ever more sure that her marriage would be a happy one.

But Walter Vandermeer, as a husband, was to prove a sore test for even the most patient and prepared woman. After a brief honeymoon at Niagara Falls, which was Jennifer's first time away from home, and which occasioned her first intimate pleasures with a man, the two newlyweds moved right back in with Poppa Schuyler. Jennifer never could figure out why her father, who was supporting the two of them, wasn't outraged by the arrangement. A man ought to support his wife, no? But her father didn't seem to mind footing the bills, not even after Peter was born. Walter earned money now and then as a handyman and part-time laborer, but mostly he got along by his winning ways with his father-in-law. To Jennifer's constant exasperation, her father and her husband would often go out drinking together, leaving her home with her infant son. Or, if they stayed home, they'd talk mostly to each other, often about Walter's plans for acquiring great wealth. Jennifer's father loved to hear these plans and usually expressed interest in "staking" him.

But none of Walter's schemes—not the one for raising sheep in a nearby field, not the one to start up a "much-needed" magazine, "Scions of Holland"—ever transgressed into the realm of action.

And when, early in 1862, Walter volunteered to join the Union Army, Jennifer was convinced it was for no other reason than to avoid family responsibility.

Perhaps it was. But Walter was not quite so cavalier about his station in life as Jennifer thought. Based in Ohio and confronted by precious little fighting (until, that is, Confederate General John Morgan invaded the state), Walter apparently had much time to think about what he would be doing when the war ended.

One day, Jennifer received a letter from him, written in highly excitable script: "Dear Jenny," it read, "Have you read about the Homestead Act? It gives veterans 160 acres of Kansas land for only ten dollars! And all the homesteader has to do to keep the land is live on it for five years! And I'll be a veteran!..."

So now, of all things, Walter wanted to be a farmer. Well, Jennifer was glad to receive that letter because now when her husband arrived home on leave, busting with with his usual enthusiasm about his plans, she would be ready for him.

And, indeed, she told him, "Walter, I see no point in discussing such a ludicrous idea. You don't know anything about farming."

"It's a desert out there," added Jennifer's father, for once not taking his son-in-law's side. "And Kansas got naked savages running around..."

Walter was taken aback by, and not a little disappointed in, his father-in-law's reaction. Still, Walter was adamant. "Now, look," he said as calmly as he could, "I've studied the matter thoroughly, and Kansas is not a desert. It's grassland. And the mad Indians are much farther out on the plains, which isn't where we're going. And, finally, I'm not so ignorant about farming—I once worked on one. So all I need is fourteen hundred dollars to outfit the family."

Jennifer's father shook his head. "I'm sorry Walt, not for this . . . "

"Twelve hundred . . . "

"No, no, I can't."

"A thousand! Lend me a thousand dollars . . . "

"Walter, I just won't do it."

Jennifer let the two men talk on. Her father seemed firm and, besides, there was no reason to assume Walter would pursue this plan any more strenuously than he pursued the others.

Indeed, when Walter returned home from the army for good, and to a new baby girl, he talked a lot on the subject but did little else. Years passed that way.

But then, shortly before his fortieth birthday, Walter took a serious turn. While cleaning the house, Jennifer came across several books in a chest. One, with the profile of a buffalo on it, was entitled, *The National Wagon Road Guide*. And there were several others, all guidebooks for the would-be settler.

Once more, Jennifer felt obligated to challenge Walter, this time rallying her two small children to her side by filling their heads with all sorts of ideas.

"I don't like Indians!" Peter cried to his father.

"I don't like the desert!" wailed Emma.

Walter, glaring at his smug wife, took his children aside and told them not to worry. He even bribed them with stories of his own; that there were no schools out that way, that they'd have plenty of friends to play with, and that they'd each have a horse.

All this did the trick. "Hooray for Kansas!" shouted Peter.

"Horray for Kansas!" repeated his little sister.

This left Jennifer virtually speechless, but she was still convinced that Walter would take no further action.

But he did. Week after week, Walter went about his preparations for leaving Ohio. He added to his meager savings by working constantly at various jobs, mostly as a handyman, and as he made his money, he purchased and stacked in the corner of the parlor those things he would need for the journey: a shovel, hoe, campstool, blankets, ropes, bandages, tool box, and so forth—including even his wife's own baggage, which he had taken the liberty to pack.

And, if there was still any doubt about his intentions, he soon put that to rest. One warm spring morning, he rode up to the house in an honest-to-God prairie schooner pulled by two yokes of oxen, just like the wagons Jennifer had seen in her *Harper's Weekly*. The schooner's arching top scraped the lane's overhanging tulip tree branches. The children from the neighborhood came running and climbed all over the wagon. Peter and Emma were very proud.

"Walter, I can't believe you actually . . ." started Jennifer as she emerged from the house and stood on the porch.

Walter just sat way up there on the seat, reins in hand,

and glared silently down at his wife as if to say, "Believe it."

Jennifer descended the two planks from the porch and slowly walked around the wagon to inspect it. Soon, neighbors were stepping outside their houses for a look. A few approached the wagon. "Say, Walt, I guess you're serious about leaving," said one of them, puffing on a long, slender pipe while standing back and sizing up the schooner.

"I guess I am, Charley," said Walter, following Jennifer with his eyes as she walked around the front of the oxen, who were snorting through black, runny nostrils. "We're heading out in a couple of weeks."

Upon hearing this, Jennifer headed for the porch again, quickening her pace to reach the house before she burst into tears.

From that night on, Jennifer pleaded with her husband to change his mind. Her father, too, sat down with Walter several times to discuss the matter. Jennifer counted on her father. At least he wouldn't start crying if he became too frustrated. And Walter respected his opinion.

Unfortunately, Walter, this time, was resolute. He often stormed out of the house rather than listen. Still, Jennifer didn't give up hope. She had faith in her father's persuasive efforts—until, that is, one terrible, rainy night.

It was late, past midnight, and Jennifer had gone to bed, leaving the two men in the parlor before a fire to discuss the move, which was only one week away at that point. But Jennifer couldn't sleep, and she tiptoed down the creaky stairs to listen to her father and husband talking in the parlor, just as she used to tiptoe down to listen to her parents talk when her mother was alive.

The two men spoke quietly so as not awaken anyone, and Jennifer had to press her head close to the glass-paned doors.

"Look, Walter, won't you reconsider?"

"Fred, I've told you a million times that there's nothing to reconsider. I'm going."

"But she's my only daughter, my only child. I don't think I can bear the thought of her out there in the wilds of Kansas. I don't care what you say about the Indians. They like white women."

"Look, do you think I would do anything to hurt her? I tell you, this is all for the best. I've got to make something of my life. People talk."

"Is that the reason you're going? Hell, let them talk. What do you care, suddenly?"

"I care because they're right. Fred, my children are getting older and smarter, and I don't want them to grow up thinking their father's a no-account."

There was a pause.

"You're a strange man, Walt. I never knew you felt such things."

"I do."

"Still, isn't there any way to dissuade you?"

"No, I'm afraid not."

Another pause.

"Well, you should've come right out and told me all this sooner. I can understand how you feel—mind you, I still don't like the idea—but I can understand."

"That's good enough."

"Hell, I guess even, well, I guess even I'm a little proud of you."

"Thanks, Fred. That means a lot to me."

There was a long silence. "Then go, Walt. God be with you."

Jennifer still shuddered when she recalled those words, "God be with you." A wave of fury came over her as she sat before Walter's grave. She had always counted on her father to protect her, to speak out for her—but just when she needed him most...

The sun was now slipping into the grass on the western

horizon. The sky, however, was flat and grey and didn't blush with the usual color. Jennifer rose to her feet and brushed her skirt. It was best to go before it got too dark to see. She looked toward the wagon and ox. Beyond was the inviting East. She closed her eyes a moment and followed the wagon wheel ruts back over the eastern horizon...

Dipping here, rising there, crinkling, flattening out, treeless but for those rare clefts of sheltered streambeds lined with willows, the prairie she had crossed in her bone-jarring wagon journey rolled back before her shut lids like a magic lantern show. Once more she saw that miserable highway, posted with the grave markers of would-be settlers and strewn with the discarded relics of civilization: a table here, a chair there, even a harmonium at one spot. She remembered painfully how some of her own furniture—her embroidered ottoman, her dresser, porch chairs—had to be jettisoned during a heavy rain so that the oxen, led by Walter, who often went on foot to further lighten the beasts' burden, could haul the wagon through the mud.

Once more she came to the spot where Walter, again on foot, led the oxen and wagon off the path to let by a creaky and dilapidated prairie schooner returning eastward. The driver, unshaven and drawn, didn't stop to talk, but nodded blankly as he passed. When the wagons had cleared each other, Jennifer, sitting alone on the seat, looked back into the rear of the receding schooner and saw a cluster of silent, hollow-eyed children staring back at her. Where was their mother?

Jennifer shook off that terrible memory and quickened her return journey. Farther east, the prairie was more lush, and the grasses grew so tall that they had nearly swallowed up Jennifer's prairie schooner, but for its arching cloth covering. Standing on the ground and looking up at the swaying grass tops, she had felt as if she were a tiny insect in a giant's backyard, and she almost expected to see on the horizon a monstrously large, white, picket fence rising up into the heavens. How painfully slow had been the wagon's progress through those grasses! The days came and went, the wagon's wheels turned and turned, but always the same grass-scape and big sky made it seem as if the Vandermeers hadn't progressed at all; that no matter how far they went, they remained in the same spot.

Now, however, in her mind's eye, Jennifer could fly as fast as she wished: back past the rolling Missouri hills, swaths of furrowed fields, farm houses and windmills, across the barge-filled Mississippi to the Illinois side, whereupon she dashed through better rooted prairie communities of schoolhouses and church spires, until the trail brought her back to a border of tall sunflowers, whose bright, orange faces signaled the end of the grasslands. Behind them was the tangled screen of gnarly crabapple and sumac, and behind them at last the great eastern forest, which cloaked the vast sky with a leafy canopy all the way to the Wabash River and the awaiting Indiana shore, where macadamized roads and ever more villages prompted Jennifer on to her Ohio...

But before Jennifer could find her own bosky lane, her reverie was broken. The ox had lowed fretfully. Jennifer opened her eyes. The air was darker. The ox stamped its hooves, tossed its head, and snorted as it tried to back up, fighting the wagon wheel break. Jennifer spun and looked about. She gasped.

Trotting in the gloom among the infringing grasses and tilted headstones were the grey, shadowy forms of wolves.

Chapter Five
Wolf Country

Her eyes wide and darting from one shadowy form to another, Jennifer backed slowly toward the wagon. She dared not make any sudden move. Walter had once told her and the children, "If wolves ever come upon you in the open, don't run. It'll only trigger them to attack."

For now, the wolves seemed calm. Indeed, they hardly acknowledged Jennifer or the ox. They sniffed around the headstones, a few pawed at the fresh dirt over Walter's grave, and one wolf, its tail held high, urinated on an inscribed plank. Other wolves disappeared and reappeared in the tall grasses, which were beginning to wave in a growing wind, unveiling previously hidden grave markers at the edges of the cemetery.

Standing beside the wagon now, Jennifer counted the wolves—two, three, four, five—But each time she thought she counted the whole pack, other wolves appeared—eight, nine, ten—

The ox lowed fitfully and shoved the wagon backward, the unyielding wagon wheel skidding a foot along the ground. Jennifer grabbed the wagon and pulled herself up onto the seat. From her higher vantage point, she could see, to her horror, still more wolf heads threading through the blowing grasses around the cemetery. One wolf rolled around on its back, then rose to its feet and sniffed the flattened spot. Two others chased and growled at each other. Yet another, its ears perked, its eyes locked onto the ground, seemed to be stalking something small, like a rodent.

The sun had now nearly set, and everything was fading into a dark greyness. Jennifer reached down into the jockey box at her feet. As a homesteader, Walter always tried to be prepared, and she prayed he had his old Army .45 down there. Though she had never fired a gun, she was prepared to do so now. Perhaps even the mere sound of a shot would scare the pack away.

She rummaged through the box. Its contents were still visible. There was a hammer, some beef jerky, a tin of tobacco, bullets even, but no gun. There was, however, a coal oil lantern and matches. Jennifer removed the lantern and lit it. The glow spread slowly out, recasting pale light upon the ground. Headstones reemerged from the gloom. Some of the near wolves, their attention caught by the lantern, lowered their heads, as if trying to see under the light. Their eyes glowed eerily. Jennifer hung the lantern on a bent nail embedded in the jockey box. But as she lifted the reins and raised her eyes, terror gripped her. She couldn't believe what she saw. Swarming in the grasses outside the cemetery were still more glowing pairs of eyes, almost like fireflies in the summer evening. It seemed to Jennifer she was surrounded by at least fifty or sixty wolves.

The ox raised its head and lowed into the starless sky. Jennifer gently flicked the reins. The ox tried to move forward, only to struggle against the wagon wheel break. Flustered, Jennifer released it. She flicked the reins again. "Go," she hissed. The ox tried to bolt, but Jennifer held him to a walk. One wolf that had been lying down in front jumped to its feet and trotted out of the way.

The wagon rolled down the little hill on a nearly invisible, narrow trail. The lantern swung, throwing swelling and shrinking shadows upon the grass, teeming with wolves. No matter how far the wagon went, no matter which way she looked, Jennifer saw still more wolves. Nearby, they were grey and shadowy. Farther off, they were only those glowing eyes.

The pack seemed endless. But Jennifer realized it really wasn't. Rather, it was following the wagon. This wasn't obvious at first because the wolves just seemed to be there at every stretch of the way. But then Jennifer lifted her lantern to extend the range of its light, and she saw that she was the hub of a moving pack, some of whose members trotted alongside the wagon, others of whom ran ahead to wait for the wagon to catch up. Jennifer wondered why the wolves didn't attack. Surely a fat ox and a not-so-fat woman were tempting enough prey. All she could figure, and hope for, was that they had already eaten.

She returned the lantern to the bent nail. Her eyes watered. She pictured her children as orphans stranded so far from home. A tear dribbled down her cheek. She was sorely tempted to set the ox running, but she knew he would never outdistance wolves.

One troublemaker began to worry her. He was a skinny thing, and he kept nipping at the ox's rear left hoof. The ox didn't seem to notice, or—if oxen were so capable—he was choosing to ignore the pest. But it was only a matter of time, thought Jennifer, before the wolf took a real bite. Then the ox would lunge, and the hunt would be on.

Jennifer continued steadfastly through the grass until she came to the clear rutted trail that lead to the Baker homestead. Along this trail she rode at the same slow rate, ever accompanied by her horrific escorts. It seemed like an eternity, but Jennifer at last saw in the black distance a solitary light, a beacon: the Baker soddy.

Again, Jennifer was tempted to flick the reins and make a dash for it, screaming as she went. Then Seth Baker might come out with his rifle and shoot at the wolves. But even as she considered this, she knew it would as likely be suicidal for her.

Then she noticed something—the grasses were empty. The wolves were gone.

Jennifer turned in every direction. She raised the lantern over her head. She saw nothing within its glow now but the billowing sea-like waves of grass, beneath which, so it seemed, the wolf pack had plunged to some greater depth.

Later, as Jennifer arrived at the Baker soddy, her heart racing, she noted two wagons and two mules tied up outside. Through the parted red window curtains she saw some of the neighbors who had been to the burial. Only now did she start feeling safe. Even so, before stepping down, she looked about to see if the wolves were stalking her. She saw mostly the night, except where the soddy's light was illuminating the ground, the horses, and the elm's rough trunk.

But Jennifer was still reluctant to get off the wagon. She listened. She heard the murmuring voices inside the soddy and the wind blowing across the unseen expanse. And still she couldn't help but feel that the wolves were hunkering down in the grass just waiting for her to come within reach. She was angry that no one had heard her wagon pull up, and she was tempted to call out. But then she'd feel like the hysterical fool. So, summoning her courage, she lowered herself from the wagon, tied the ox to the hitching post alongside another wagon, and hurried in, carrying the lantern with her.

"Jennifer, we were about to send out a search party for you," scolded Lucy, hurrying over to the door.

Jennifer, her body trembling, craned her neck and surveyed

the dimly lit room, which was hardly bigger than her own dugout and just as cramped, especially with all the guests. The low ceiling, made of brush, was kept up by long pole beams. A section in the middle was covered by cheese cloth, perhaps to decorate the ceiling, or perhaps to keep dirt from sprinkling onto the table. The windows were hung with red calico curtains, the walls were plastered, and there was a fireplace, which was constructed like the rest of the house, from blocks of sod. "Peter and Emma," said Jennifer, "where are they?"

Lucy had barely pointed to them in a corner, talking with her own three children, when Jennifer dashed to them, her eyes overflowing with tears. She crouched, putting the lantern on the hard floor, and she embraced and rocked them while the Baker children and the adults watched. One of the neighbors stepped up behind her.

"My wife, Hattie, sends her sympathies," he said in a deep, hoarse voice. "She's laid up and couldn't come."

Jennifer rose to her feet and wiped her cheek with her fingers. Standing before her was the square-built, older man with short, white hair she had first seen in Franz Hoffmann's store.

"There were wolves," she began. "So many wolves . . . "

The square-built man raised his white eyebrows. "Did they bother you?"

"I've never imagined there could be so many at once . . . "

"They are unnerving," agreed Lucy, stepping forward. "But you're all right now." She led Jennifer to the rough-hewn table in the center of the room. "You just sit and eat something. We've got fresh prairie chicken and plenty of cornbread."

Nancy's lanky husband, Will, quickly rose from his seat at the table and offered it to Jennifer. "Excuse me," he said, his prominent Adam's apple rising and falling along his slender throat.

Jennifer sat, but was distracted. "Have the children? . . . "

"They ate a while ago," said Lucy, hurrying to the fireplace. "Tend to yourself now."

"Awfully sorry about your husband," said Will, backing awkwardly out of Lucy's way.

"They were all around me," continued Jennifer. "I thought surely they were going to attack. I felt so—vulnerable."

"Yeah, there are no trees to climb, and you can't outrun them," said the square-built man, trying to find a place to sit. "By the way, my name's Aaron. Aaron Whittaker."

"Still, I prefer wolves to a certain person," said Seth Baker, straddling a chair.

"Uh-huh, getting back to that," said Aaron Whittaker, "like I was saying, I talked to a few people, and they agree with me . . . "

Jennifer wondered what they were all suddenly referring to. It seemed as if her presence had interrupted some discussion even though, ostensibly, everyone was there to see her.

"I tell you, he's up to no good. Did you know he's been sending homesteaders away?"

"Oh, stop and think a moment, will you? He's a government land agent!"

"Yeah, and he seems to own most of the land in town! I tell you, he's got something cooking!"

"With the railroad?"

"And the cattle interests, yes . . . "

Jennifer only barely listened. She felt uneasy, realizing that Nancy Camp had been standing off aways and staring at her solemnly with her big, doe-like eyes. Lucy, meanwhile, set a plate down before her. "I'll fetch you some coffee," she said. Jennifer tried to eat, but she had no appetite.

Finally, Nancy Camp approached the table. She sat down cater-cornered to Jennifer. "How are you feeling?" she asked, touching Jennifer's hand.

"Those wolves . . . "

"I know. Sometimes their howls keep me awake at night."

"It seems to me he oughtn't be a land agent then," growled Aaron Whittaker.

"I say we all go into town the first thing in the morning to talk with him," said Lucy to everyone as she brought Jennifer her coffee.

"I agree," said Will. "Let's confront him on this!"

"Perhaps he thinks we're blind to him," said Lucy, "or maybe that farm folk are stupid."

Nancy shook her head in admiration. "Will you listen to her? My, I wish I were as strong. She's been gabbing with the men all evening about that Bill Wilkes." Nancy stopped to listen again.

"No one made him king," Lucy was saying. "This is farming land, not range."

"I tell you," remarked Nancy quietly, leaning close to Jennifer, "I, for one couldn't address a group of men like that."

"Well, there are a lot of things I cannot do," said Jennifer, gazing down at her coffee. "Which is why I'll be returning to Ohio."

Nancy looked at her neighbor as if unprepared for such an announcement. "Oh, dear, you don't mean it."

"Why, yes, of course . . ."

"Just because you saw some wolves . . ."

"There weren't just 'some' . . ."

"I was hoping we might become better acquainted. It can be so very lonely on this prairie without another woman to talk to."

Jennifer was taken aback by this sudden show of interest on the part of her neighbor. "You have Lucy."

"Yes, and I love her," said Nancy. "But sometimes she can be difficult. She's just so strong. She doesn't always understand how I feel. You do. You're like me."

Jennifer was sorry she had said anything to Nancy about leaving. The last thing she needed was to have someone try to talk her out of it. "It was not my idea to leave Ohio. And now that Walter is . . . gone . . . "

"What does it matter whose idea it was? You're here now."

"I miss my father."

"We all miss someone . . . "

Jennifer's eyes glazed over. "God, I don't know how I'll tell him about Walter."

"Why, we can become like sisters," continued Nancy. "Wouldn't that be nice? We can share secrets. I can't do that with Lucy. Please, Jenny, say you won't go."

"I had better write him first," said Jennifer. "Hm! He'll see now that I was right. I trust he won't ever side against me again."

"Jenny, are you listening to me?" Nancy pushed forward from her chair and gripped Jennifer's wrist. "You know, Lucy likes you. I can tell."

"Nancy, I . . . "

"She'd miss you."

Jennifer turned her head away. "I have no husband. It's impossible . . . "

"No, it's not. Lucy was already suggesting that you might teach school. Would you like that?"

"Teach school?"

"Yes. Why, you'd be a very important lady around here."

Jennifer shook her head. "The very idea . . . "

"Oh, please don't say no. At least think about it."

Jennifer was about to explain her position some more, but she didn't have the energy for it, especially since Nancy seemed almost panicky. It was much easier to tell her neighbor what she wanted to hear. "All right. I'll think about it."

Nancy brightened. "You'll see," she said, leaning back in her chair and feeling she had won at least a temporary victory. "You'll get along just fine. Lucy and I will see to it."

Jennifer gazed at the cornbread on her plate. Why, she

wondered, does everyone try to tell me what to do? Is it so obvious to them all how weak I am?

Nancy and Jennifer didn't exchange another word on the subject, each fearing what the other might say. They listened to the ongoing conversation.

"The railroad ought to be a good thing," Will Camp was saying. "But not if it's going to drive us out."

"No one is driving us out," said Seth.

"Yeah? And what if they bring cattle up here?" asked Will.

Jennifer tried to pay attention, but now she kept getting distracted by two men in suspenders, who hadn't been speaking at all. They were just leaning against a wall. But while one was at least listening attentively to the discussion, the other was staring at her. Only when Jennifer dared look directly at him did he avert his eyes. Jennifer remembered the two men from that afternoon. They were the brothers who buried Walter. The one who kept staring at her was the younger one. He looked at Jennifer again with dark, piercing eyes, and this time it was she who averted her eyes. He pushed off the wall and, hat in hand, stepped up to her.

"I'm sorry about your husband, ma'am, Mrs. Vandermeer," he said in a low, slow voice.

Jennifer forced herself to look up at his intense face. "Thank you."

"I reckon you have no man now to help you with your chores."

"No, I don't."

"I'd be pleased to come by your homestead and help out."

"Why, thank you, but it's not necessary."

The dark-haired man looked at his feet. "You have nothing that needs fixing?"

"No, that is, it doesn't matter . . . "

"You have meat? I can hunt you some meat."

"Really, sir, you're most kind, but . . . "

"Name's Joseph, ma'am. Joseph Caulder. That's my

brother, Isaac, by the wall.'' Isaac, who had silver in his hair and a softer, more worn, face, held his chin up high as if it let him better hear the discussion in the room.

"I'm pleased to know you, Mr. Caulder," said Jennifer, "but I don't want you to waste your time."

"Oh, I wouldn't be wasting it. Things are slow at our place."

Jennifer felt her resistance sapping. "Mr. Caulder . . . ''

"You can call me Joseph."

"Joseph. If you insist, I won't say no . . . ''

"Then I'll be by."

Not a glimmer of a smile creased Joseph's mouth. He simply nodded and returned to his brother.

"Do you see?" whispered Nancy. "I'm not the only one who wants you to stay."

Jennifer was about to try to explain but then the room stirred. The discussion had ended. Everyone was making for the door.

Before leaving, however, each person stopped by Jennifer to do what they had originally come for, pay their condolences. Jennifer rose to her feet to meet them.

"Hattie'll catch you another time," said Aaron Whittaker, stopping before her.

"I know," said Jennifer. "I hope she feels better soon."

Aaron stepped into the night air and put his hat on.

"If you need anything . . . '' said Will Camp, Nancy on his arm.

"I'll be fine, thank you," said Jennifer.

"Please think over what we talked about," said Nancy, turning her head as she left with her husband.

Jennifer didn't answer.

Isaac Caulder passed her, wearing a straw hat. "God protect you," he muttered, only half-looking at Jennifer as he continued out.

His brother, Joseph, however, hat still in hand, stopped.

"I may be a little late, ma'am," he said, "but I'll be there."

Jennifer stiffened. "You needn't rush, Mr. Caulder. Really." "It's Joseph, if you please. And it's no trouble at all." He then joined his brother outside.

Seth and Lucy saw their guests out. Jennifer was left in the room, listening to Peter and Emma talking in the corner with the three Baker children, the younger two of whom, Jeremy and Mary, were barefoot. Jennifer remembered how Walter one evening in their dugout had suggested that their own children go barefoot "so we won't seem like uppity people." But Jennifer wouldn't hear of it, and it was one of the few times she had gotten her way.

"Well! The place certainly seems larger with everyone gone!" remarked Lucy, returning with her arm around Seth's waist, and his arm around hers.

"I knew a fellow once," added Seth, his pale grey eyes twinkling, "who used to bring his cows and pigs into his soddy just so he could kick them out again and feel he lived in a palace."

Lucy smiled at her husband's story, but Jennifer couldn't manage it, not even to be polite.

"You hardly ate," said Lucy, noting the full plate on the table.

"It was tasty, thank you. I'm just not hungry."

"Momma!" called out Emma from the corner. "Todd's got an Indian scalp!"

Todd Baker, sitting with the younger children, slumped and looked to the sod wall, shaking his head.

Lucy put her hands on her hips and stared squarely at her teenaged son across the room. "Todd Baker! What stories are you telling them?"

"Aw, she heard wrong," said Todd.

"I did not!" returned Emma, hurrying over to Jennifer. "He showed it to us!"

"Scalps! Goodness!" said Jennifer.

"It's just a swatch of buffalo fur," said Seth quietly to Jennifer, smirking at his son's joke.

"Just for lying, young man," said Lucy, "you will go to bed early with the young ones."

"She heard wrong!" insisted Todd, lifting his head pleadingly.

"I didn't!" said Emma. "Ask anyone."

"That's what he told us," confirmed Jeremy Baker with satisfaction.

Todd made as if to give his brother the back of his hand.

"Todd!" shouted Lucy.

"Aw, I wasn't going to hit him."

"Don't even pretend," said Lucy sternly. "Now, off to bed! All of you!"

In short order, the children washed up and went to bed. They shared two hay mattresses—Todd, Jeremy, and Peter were squeezed into one; and Mary and Emma had the other. A blanket hung from one of the pole beams to block the grownup's light from disturbing them. "Maw, it's too early," complained Todd from behind the curtain. "I can't sleep."

"That will teach you to raise a hand to your brother," responded Lucy, sitting at the table with Jennifer over some tea. "Now, hush!"

Seth, meanwhile, sat himself in a corner and was cleaning his rifle. He kept whistling some indeterminate melody.

"Todd is not a bad boy," explained Lucy.

"I know," said Jennifer.

Lucy took a sip from her cup. "How do you like the tea?"

"It's quite good."

"It's horse mint. I have the children gather it every summer. Would you like to take some home with you? I have plenty."

"Thank you, I still have tea I brought with me from the east."

Lucy took another sip. "Well, what did you and Nancy talk about? Your plans, I take it."

"Yes. I'm afraid she's insisting I stay in Kansas."

"Well, certainly, I feel the same way."

Jennifer fell silent.

"You weren't intending to return to Ohio, were you?"

"Lucy, of course I was."

Lucy shook her head to dismiss the idea. "There's no reason to. You have a hundred and sixty acres of land and a home."

"They were Walter's acres. I'm not going to till it. And my home is a badger hole."

Lucy fixed her dark grey eyes on Jennifer. "I assume Nancy told you about the possibility of your teaching school."

"She did, but I couldn't . . ."

"We have no teacher in these parts. Never have. We do our best to educate our children, but it's not the same. I fear Todd isn't as strong in his letters as he ought to be."

"Lucy, I'm flattered that you should ask . . ."

"You seem well educated . . ."

"But I have no experience teaching."

"Let's have no 'buts.' You needn't decide now anyway. I ask only that you think about it."

"Yes, I told Nancy I would do that much."

"I mean, think about it seriously."

"Yes, I will."

"Fine. Nancy and I will come by your place tomorrow afternoon to discuss it at greater length—that is, of course, unless you wish to stay here at our home longer. You are entirely welcome to do so."

"No, thank you, but it's not necessary."

Lucy leaned back. "May I get you more tea?"

"No, I'm fine," said Jennifer, already rehearsing how she would tell the two women that she would not be teaching.

For the rest of the evening Lucy didn't press her point,

and there were moments for Jennifer when she was truly comforted in her grief by the domesticity of the room. While Seth continued to lavish attention on his rifle, whistling his vague melody, Lucy and Jennifer talked of various things. Surprised at Lucy's interests, Jennifer told her what the latest fashions were back east, at least as far east as Ohio, and she promised to show Lucy some of her own finer dresses and hoops, which were still packed. Then Lucy told Jennifer some of her favorite recipes, especially her preserves made from globe apples, virtually the only fruit within foot gathering distance. Then Jennifer asked how Lucy got the floor to be so hard, and Lucy told her she sprinkled salt into the dirt. By and by, though, Lucy signaled her tiredness with a yawn. "Well, I think that's enough oil burned for one evening."

"Yep, I'm about through here," said Seth from his corner, squinting down the barrel of his rifle.

So the three prepared for sleep, and soon Lucy and Jennifer were sharing the Baker's mattress while displaced Seth rolled up cheerfully in a buffalo rug on the floor.

But Jennifer had trouble falling asleep. She felt uncomfortable lying in someone else's bed, and too much had happened to her. So she gazed into the blackness and listened to Seth's snoring compete with the wind outside.

But she did fall asleep eventually, and she even dreamed.

She found herself resuming her eastward trek to Ohio. Only this time she managed to reach all the way to her porch and hurry right into her house. There she went about her housekeeping duties for her father, just as she had done years ago, before she ever met Walter. Her father sat in his usual chair, reading the paper and grumbling. She felt at peace—until she heard distant howling. "They followed me," she said, rising from her rocker. She returned to the porch and looked out onto the benighted lane. She grew frightened. Out there she saw a long line of wolves sitting side-by-side and sending their woeful cries up into the unseen branches of the tulip trees.

Chapter Six
A Popular Woman

The next morning, Jennifer and her children had breakfast with the Bakers. Everyone crowded around the rough-hewn table and ate flapjacks, eggs, salt pork and, best of all, milk, which was a scarce commodity around the Vandermeer homestead, since Walter hadn't acquired a cow. Jennifer was glad to see her children drink the milk.

Afterward, while Seth and Todd went into the field, Jennifer, Lucy, and the rest of the children brought the breakfast dishes outside and washed them in a large wooden tub. It was almost festive as the Baker children splashed each other. Peter and Emma caught some water, but they didn't splash back, being subdued from the loss of their father. Noting this, Lucy scolded her children to stop.

Later, the children marched back into the soddy with the dishes, and Jennifer announced that she would be returning to her dugout.

"Are you sure you're all right?" asked Lucy, remaining outside and wiping her hands on her apron.

"I'll be fine," said Jennifer, rolling down her sleeves. "Thank you for your hospitality."

"Very well. But Nancy and I will be by this afternoon to

see how you're doing—and to discuss that teaching matter."

Jennifer turned toward the soddy. "Peter! Emma! Come, we're leaving!"

Emma, barefoot like her little friends, stepped outside. "Do we have to?"

"Yes, we have to! And put your shoes on!"

"It looks like Emma and Mary are becoming friends," commented Lucy.

"It would seem so," said Jennifer.

"I think Mary looks up to your daughter a little."

"Well, Emma is a year older, and a year is a lot at their age."

"And I think it's the same with our boys. Peter is nearly two years older than Jeremy."

Peter and Emma emerged from the soddy, Emma's shoes now on.

The two children climbed into the back of the wagon, and Jennifer untied the ox. As she climbed up on the wagon seat, Lucy said, "Wait, just a minute." She hurried into her soddy. Jennifer waited. Off in the distance she could see Seth and Todd toiling in the field. A moment later, Lucy returned with a gunnysack and handed it to Jennifer. "Some provisions. You were so awfully low when I was at your place."

Jennifer peeked inside. She saw some bread, salt pork, dried fruit, vegetables, and she smelled horsemint tea. "Thank you, I'll repay your kindness." She placed the sack behind her with her children, gripped the reins, and started the ox away from the soddy.

"I'll see you later," said Lucy, raising her voice, her children coming to her side.

Jennifer directed the ox straight through the wild grass, taking the short cut Lucy had shown her, scaring into flight a flock of sparrows.

When Jennifer arrived back at her homestead, she was

startled to see a man plowing the field with two of her oxen. It was as if Walter's ghost had returned to finish his work. Jennifer rode the wagon up to the man and saw whom she suspected it was. "Why, Mr. Caulder—Joseph," she said, "you're early."

Joseph Caulder stopped the plow and squinted up at Jennifer. "Yes, ma'am," he said in his low, slow voice. "I guess I am."

"I wish you had waited," said Jennifer. "Honest, I don't expect to farm this land."

"This ain't for crops ma'am. I'm plowing a fire-break. When I'm done here, I'll tend to that wagon axle." Joseph's face didn't show a glimmer of a smile. "It needs greasing."

"Yes, it's been like that."

Joseph turned back to the plow to resume his work.

"When you're done, Joseph, come to the dugout. I'll prepare you some lunch."

"Much obliged, ma'am," said Joseph as the two oxen pulled the plow forward.

"And I wish you'd call me Jennifer."

"Yes, ma'am—Jennifer."

Jennifer watched him move off. She shook her head. Mr. Caulder was an amusing man. She flicked the reins and continued on to her dugout, where Joseph had tied up his grey-muzzled mule. "Start packing, children," she said, pulling up on the reins.

"Packing, Momma?" asked Emma.

"We're going home."

"To Ohio?"

"That's right." Jennifer descended from the wagon. Her children jumped off the back, Emma lugging the gunnysack. Jennifer decided she would leave her furniture behind. Let her neighbors fight over her rocker, her table and chairs, her cookstove. She meant to travel light and fast. She wondered if she might exchange the oxen for some horses.

Perhaps Mr. Turner, the blacksmith, could help her.

Meanwhile, she and her children began packing up their possessions: clothing, dishes, a few curios, toys—along the way she came upon the slender blue volume of *Bridal Greetings*. She paused to leaf through it. "Peace to thee, fair and gentle bride! Thou art now joined to the soul for whom thine was moulded. Blessings rest on thy head." Jennifer nearly cried as she closed the book, placing it gently in a crate.

Shortly before noon she was in the midst of putting her silverware into a crate when Joseph, sweating, straw hat in hand, appeared in the open doorway, blocking some of the light.

"Oh, Joseph, is it lunch time already?" asked Jennifer. "I'm sorry, I lost track of time. I'll make you something."

"Didn't come up for that," he said. "Just thought you'd like to know you got company coming up the trail."

"Goodness, that would be Lucy and Nancy," said Jennifer, hurrying to the window.

"No, it's not them," said Joseph. "It's Karl Pfeffer. He's the only one in these parts who owns a buggy. He lives south of here."

Jennifer looked out the window and saw, sure enough, a solitary figure riding up the trail from the opposite direction of town in a buggy. She stepped outside, followed by Emma. The buggy, pulled by a dark brown horse, soon pulled off the trail and headed up to the dugout. On the side of the buggy were big, fancy letters that read, "Studebaker."

"Hello," greeted Jennifer. Emma stayed by her mother, curious to see this new neighbor.

"Goot afternoon," said Karl Pfeffer, pulling up on the reins. "Vhy, hello, Joe," he added, noting Joseph Caulder standing by the dugout.

"Karl," returned Joseph flatly.

Karl Pfeffer, a heavy-set man in his fifties, lowered himself to the ground with some effort. He was dressed as if going to church, with a dark hat, tight-fitting suit, and a tie pin—no tie—in the middle of his shirt. "Mrs. Vandermeer, I beliefe," he said, removing his hat, revealing thick, silver hair combed back.

"Yes, said Jennifer.

Karl Pfeffer's eyes suddenly softened. "Ach! Zuch a delicate flower in dis vilderness, eh, Jozeph?"

Joseph screwed up his face uncomfortably. "I reckon."

"Ah! Und who is dis?" said Pfeffer, stooping slightly. "Emma, maybe?"

Emma was squinting shyly at him from behind her mother's skirt. Jennifer stroked her daughter's dark hair. "Say hello to Mr. Pfeffer."

"Ach, zo you already know my name," said Karl Pfeffer. "Goot."

"Hello," peeped Emma.

Karl Pfeffer gave a laugh. "Und your boy? Peter is his name? Is he about?"

"He's just inside," said Jennifer. "Peter! Come out and say hello to Mr. Pfeffer!"

Peter appeared silently in the doorway.

"Ah. Der he is. Hello, Peter! Zuch lovely blonde hair."

"Yes—um, Mr. Pfeffer," said Jennifer, a little confused, "is this a social visit?"

Karl Pfeffer returned his attention to Jennifer. "Vell, I did come to speak vit you—but if Joe vould excuse us, it's radder private."

Joseph straightened tensely.

"Is it," said Jennifer awkwardly.

"That's all right," said Joseph. "I'll go finish the firebreak."

"Thank you, Joseph," said Jennifer. "Then do come back, and I'll prepare your lunch."

Joseph nodded and started back to the awaiting oxen and plow.

"See you later, Joe," called Karl, holding his hat slightly aloft. Joseph acknowledged him with another quick nod and continued on.

"He's offered to help around here," explained Jennifer.

"So I see. He's quite der gentleman."

"Shall we go inside?"

"Let's."

"Peter, you stay outside with your sister," said Jennifer, nudging her son from the doorway. "Come in, Mr. Pfeffer."

Karl Pfeffer stepped inside the dingy, cramped dugout. "A fine little home you haff here, Mrs. Vandermeer."

"You're being kind. It's just a cave."

"Not to your liking?"

"Hardly. Please, sit." Karl Pfeffer sat by the table, his pot belly extending over his belt. "May I offer you something? Tea?"

"Don't go to any bodder. Pleaze take a chair yourzelf."

Jennifer sat down, and the two faced each other beside the table. Karl Pfeffer furrowed his heavy brow as if in serious thought.

"Is something the matter?" asked Jennifer.

His brow relaxed. Karl Pfeffer looked squarely at Jennifer. "Mrs. Vandermeer, I hope you'll excuse me if I zeem a little forvard—dat is, blunt."

"Please, go right ahead."

"T'ank you. Mrs. Vandermeer, fife years ago I lost my vife, Hilda—God rest her zoul—to a smallpox epidemic. It ravaged der whole countryzide, took many Indians vit it. Anyvay, I've zince been living on my farm vit my two daughters and zon, all of dem grown. Dey're fine company—vell-behaved und respectful—but it can still be lonely vit'out a vife."

"I know what you mean."

"I t'ought you might. Now, vomen—dat is, unmarried

vomen—are awfully scarse around dese parts. Now, you just lost a husband, und I'm zorry to hear it. But it does create an opportunity fur a man like myzelf, if you know vhat I mean."

Jennifer felt her cheeks flush. "Actually, I'm not sure I do."

Karl Pfeffer shifted his bulk uncomfortably in his chair but kept his pale blue eyes locked intently on Jennifer. "Mrs. Vandermeer, I'fe got a goot farm, vood-frame houze, and zome money to spare fur a vife to buy her zome nice t'ings if she had a mind to. I'm a hard vorker, a goot Christian, und I don't drink . . . "

"Goodness, Mr. Pfeffer! This sounds like a marriage proposal!"

"Don't misunderstand. I fully intend to giff proper time to der courting dat a decent lady like yourzelf dezerfs. I just vanted to make sure you vere amenable to der idea. I hope I haffn't offended you."

"No, I'm flattered. I think."

"Now, like I set, my children are all grown, so dey von't be a burden to you. In fact, dey'd be a help. As fur your own zon and daughter, I'll raise dem as if dey ver my own."

"Please, Mr. Pfeffer . . . "

"Call me Karl."

"Karl, I really don't see it . . . "

"Is it my age? I can assure you, I'm a heal'ty man."

"No, it's not that."

"Der's zomeone elze maybe?"

"Certainly not! Mr. Pfeffer, my husband just died!"

Karl Pfeffer stiffened and fell silent. He took a deep breath and refurrowed his brow. "Vell, if I'm not der callous von," he grumbled. "You're right. Forgiff me."

"That's quite all right. But under the circumstances you can understand why I couldn't even begin to consider such an offer."

"Of course. It vouldn't be proper. My, you must t'ink me a real oaf."

Just then, Joseph Caulder returned, standing in the doorway, straw hat in hand.

"Oh, Joseph!" spouted Jennifer.

"Don't mean to interrupt," he said. "The fire-break's done."

Jennifer rose to her feet. "No, you're not interrupting. Come in and sit down. Mr. Pfeffer—I mean, Karl, would you like some lunch?"

Karl Pfeffer stood. He eyed Joseph suspiciously. "T'ank you, but I must get back to my place." He approached the door, and Joseph stepped aside. "It vas a pleazure meeting you."

"And it was nice to meet you," said Jennifer.

"Please, if you neet anyt'ing, anyt'ing at all, I hope you'll ask."

"Thank you, I will."

"Or if you need vork done around here, my zon und I vould be glad to oblige."

"Won't be necessary," said Joseph curtly.

Karl Pfeffer eyed his neighbor again. "Nice zeeing you too, Joe."

"Likewise."

There was a tense silence for a moment. Then Jennifer said, "Well, thank you for stopping by."

Karl Pfeffer waved his hat. "Ya, vell, don't be a stranger."

He mounted his buggy, which tilted on its leather supports, and he settled on the seat. "Good-bye, Peter, Emma!"

Peter and Emma were sitting against the well. Peter only looked up, but Emma quietly returned, "Bye."

Then Karl Pfeffer flicked his reins and rode back the way he had come. Jennifer watched him a moment, then returned to the dugout. Joseph was still standing inside.

"Won't you sit down?" asked Jennifer.

Joseph sat stiffly at the table.

Jennifer hurried to the gunnysack Lucy had given her. Then an odd thing happened. Her grieving lightened slightly, as when the sun momentarily pokes through the dark clouds. Suddenly, she found herself smiling. Never before had she been fought over by two men. And she found these two particular competitors amusing in their efforts.

"He seems like a nice man," said Jennifer as she broke out fried cakes, bacon, and coffee.

"Nice, enough," said Joseph, his face showing no emotion.

The corners of her mouth flickering into a smirk, Jennifer brought her guest his lunch and sat down at the table with him.

"He's getting kind of fat," commented Joseph sullenly.

"Oh, I hadn't noticed."

"It's from age. He's near sixty."

"I would have put him at around fifty-four or five."

"I'm forty-four, myself."

"Are you?"

Joseph bit into the cake and chewed slowly.

Jennifer's amusement, meanwhile, began to fade. Her eyes glazed over as she remembered her husband and where she was. "Tell me, Joseph, how long have you and your brother lived out here?"

Joseph swallowed. "Eight years."

"Eight years," repeated Jennifer thoughtfully. "I wonder, has anyone been around here longer than that?"

"Don't think so." Joseph took another bite of the cake.

"Was Four Corners here?"

"Just the grass." Joseph sipped the coffee.

Jennifer thought of her husband once more, then she watched the grim-faced figure sitting at her table. The man didn't smile, he didn't look up, he barely talked. Goodness! thought Jennifer. What a husband he'd make!

"I'll have to tend to the wagon axle tomorrow," said Joseph.

"Oh, I can have Peter do it."

"And I'll look at the ox stalls."

"Ox stalls?"

"Roof's falling in."

"Is it?"

"Yep."

Jennifer sat there a moment more with barely a sentence exchanged between her and her guest. It seemed to suit Joseph, but she was getting more and more uncomfortable. She kept searching for things to say.

"Warm weather."

"Yep."

"Not much rain, either."

"Nope. Not much."

"I understand winters can be very cold here."

"Some years."

Finally, Jennifer thought to call her chldren in for lunch, too, hoping to inspire some conversation. They came in and sat down, but Peter, away from the Baker children, had become morose again, and Emma, who seemed less melancholic, was nevertheless inhibited by the stern-eyed visitor. So now the four of them sat at the table with barely a word passing among them.

When Joseph at last finished his lunch and rose to his feet, Jennifer felt much relief.

"I'll be back tomorrow," he said solemnly.

"I hope you're not neglecting your own farm on my account," said Jennifer, also standing.

"Isaac's there." Joseph went outside, and Jennifer followed. He pulled himself up onto his mule. "Bye, ma'am—Jennifer." And, with that, he turned his mule about and headed off.

"He's a mean man," said Emma from the doorway.

"No, he's not," said Jennifer, her eyes following the retreating figure. "He's a kind man. He's just quiet."

"I don't like him. I like Mr. Pfeffer."

"Mr. Pfeffer is nice, too."

"He looks like Grandpoppa."

"He does, doesn't he?"

"Is he coming back?"

"Mr. Pfeffer? I imagine so."

"Mr. Caulder?"

"Him, too."

Emma frowned. "I wish he wouldn't."

"Don't be that way," said Jennifer, still watching the small, distant figure riding away.

"Who do you like better?"

"It doesn't matter," said Jennifer, turning around. "After you and your brother finish lunch, we'll resume packing."

The afternoon wore on, and Jennifer and her children spent the warmest part of the day inside the relative coolness of their dugout, packing more of their possessions. Every so often, Emma would pick up an object, like a pewter mug or candlestick, and ask, "Are we taking this?" And Jennifer would answer yes, or no. Peter, meanwhile, went about his work quietly.

Around four o'clock the packing was almost done, and Jennifer only now began to consider the seriousness of what lay ahead of her—returning across the prairie without her husband. She wasn't sure she could survive such a journey. She pictured her two children alone in the middle of the wild grasses, burying their mother. She nearly wept.

At that moment, someone knocked on the frame of the open doorway, startling her from her reverie. She spun and looked. Standing just outside, with the tawny prairie and blue sky behind them, were two most inopportune visitors.

"Afternoon, Jennifer," said Lucy, standing just in front of Nancy. Both women were wearing red sunbonnets and clasping several books to their chests. In the crook of Lucy's arm hung an unlit lantern. "May we come in?"

"Of course," said Jennifer, gesturing for them to enter,

but remembering her resolve to leave Kansas. She decided she would not speak any more than she had to. She would listen to what Lucy had to say, perhaps offer her and Nancy some tea, but then politely ask them to leave. "I must finish my packing," she would say pointedly.

"You left your lantern at my place," said Lucy, placing her books and the lantern on the table.

"Thank you," said Jennifer.

"It's so very dark in here," commented Nancy, placing her burden down, too.

"I try not to burn oil during the day," said Jennifer.

"But you may have to during school hours," said Lucy, removing her bonnet. "And you will have to clear a space for the children to sit."

"I beg your pardon," said Jennifer.

"Of course, during days like this, you could always hold class outside, but I think the children, especially the boys, might become too easily distracted. Don't you agree?"

"I wouldn't know," said Jennifer.

Lucy turned to Nancy, who had sat herself at the table and was fanning her long, sunburnt face with her hand. "We will have to tell the others to make sure Jennifer has enough oil for classes."

Nancy nodded.

"But, Lucy," said Jennifer, "aren't you getting a bit ahead of yourself? I haven't said I'm going to be teaching. In fact . . . "

"Now, don't worry, I've worked it all out. Parents will pay you what they can though you may have to accept some barter."

"Please listen, Lucy, this really is impossible. I've already decided to go home. I've been packing all day." Jennifer gestured at the various packed bags, sacks, and crates.

Lucy glimpsed them, then stared coldly at Jennifer. "But you can't," she said flatly. "Everything here has already been

arranged. Look, we've brought you some McGuffey readers.''
She patted the book stack on the table.

"And most of the children will be able to bring Bibles,''
added Nancy from her seat.

"That's all well and good,'' said Jennifer, "but I can't teach
them.''

"Sure you can,'' said Nancy, only now removing her bonnet. "And you'll be very good at it, too. You have education.''

"You don't understand. I can't stay.''

"Now see here,'' said Lucy, placing her hands on her hips,
"we rode all up and down these two prairie paths scraping
together readers from people who were not so willing to give
them up! You have an obligation, Jennifer Vandermeer, and
you should not be so quick to run out on it!''

"I—don't see that I have an obligation.''

"Don't you? This will be our first schoolhouse.''

Turning her head away, Jennifer timidly pressed the fingers
of one hand against her cheek. She wished to protest further,
but she found herself choking up.

"Lucy,'' interrupted Nancy, noticing Jennifer's distress,
"perhaps we ought to let Jenny decide this for herself.''

"Please, Nancy,'' came back Lucy hotly, "you don't have
children. I do!''

Nancy fell silent.

"Well?'' asked Lucy, returning her attention to Jennifer.
"What have you got to say?''

Jennifer lowered her head. "I want to return to Ohio.''

Lucy stood fuming. "And how do you expect to cross the
prairie?''

"I can try.''

"Try? Tell me, what would you do if you should run into
Indians? Who will protect your children?''

"You said they were harmless . . . ''

"Or bandits!''

Jennifer wiped a tear from her eye. "I don't know.''

"You don't know," repeated Lucy sarcastically. Nearly mute with frustration, she fixed her piercing gaze on Jennifer and tried to calm herself. "You realize," she resumed, "that if you wait, there may soon be a railroad spur right here in Four Corners."

Jennifer looked up. "A what?"

"That's the talk," said Lucy. "At least, it's something that Bill Wilkes has been fighting for."

"A railroad? How long before . . . "

"Within a year. Maybe by next spring."

Jennifer pictured herself aboard a train, chugging across the prairie away from Four Corners. "I wish it were here already."

"I'm sure you do. But you must be patient. Listen to me. Stay here at least until the spring. By then we should know better about the spur. In the meantime, you can teach. You might even come to like it."

"It's not really the teaching I mind . . . "

"Yes, I know. Perhaps, then, you'll become used to Kansas."

At this, Jennifer finally looked directly into Lucy's dark grey eyes. "Tell me, are you used to it?"

"I've seeded this land with two of my children," said Lucy, solemnly. "I'll never leave it."

There was now silence in the little dugout as each of the three women fell still and reflected upon different thoughts.

"I suppose," began Jennifer slowly, more to break the silence than anything, "spring will come soon enough."

Lucy, who had become darkly quiet, brightened slightly. "That's right. The months go quickly—and you'll be able to stay with Seth and me during the winter."

"Oh no, that I couldn't do . . . "

"But I won't hear otherwise," said Lucy, feeling strong again. "Winters can be harsh out here and isolate homesteads for weeks at a stretch."

Jennifer contemplated the grim prospect. Isolate homesteads? Even more than now? She shuddered.

"Besides," continued Lucy, sounding practical now, "our soddy could always use the extra body warmth. So! You'll stay?"

"Mind you, I'd only be waiting for the railroad . . ."

"Yes, yes, that's all understood," said Lucy. "Then it's settled. When would you like to begin teaching?"

Settled? thought Jennifer. Just like that? She had only been considering a possibility. She nearly protested, but she said, "Monday?"

"Monday it is! That will allow a few days for word to reach all the homesteads. And the hour?"

"Eight."

Lucy took a deep breath and began to tie her bonnet back on. "Perhaps Franz can get you a blackboard from somewhere. Come, Nancy, we have other stops to make, and then I must get home."

Nancy rose from her seat. She silently tied on her own bonnet. She seemed to be harboring some resentment, but she obediently followed Lucy out of the dugout and onto their buckboard. Lucy, apparently not noticing her friend's darkened mood, took the reins, and soon the two women were off.

Jennifer leaned against the door frame, feeling sapped of all vigor. She watched her neighbors get smaller and smaller as they cut across the grassy sea to some other homestead beyond the horizon. It was only when they were that far away that she whispered, "My God, what did I agree to?"

Chapter Seven
Sick Geraniums

Jennifer remained in the doorway several minutes more; Lucy and Nancy's buckboard was so far away, and yet it remained in sight. She marvelled at how far one could see out on the prairie.

Overhead, meanwhile, an armada of clouds drifted quickly across the sky, the white edges teased out into tatters by high winds. Soon, the vanguard of these clouds were above the distant buckboard. As they moved still farther off, the clouds met the horizon, so that it soon appeared as if the buckboard were riding right toward them.

The clouds now over Jennifer's dugout thickened. Perhaps, thought Jennifer, they'll sail all the way to Ohio. Perhaps Poppa will be reading the Gazette and hear on his window panes the patter of raindrops falling from these very clouds.

"I have a message for him," she whispered to the floating procession. "Will you take it to him?" At that moment, she realized it was time to write her father.

She waited until that evening, after Peter and Emma were tucked away in their corner. Then she brewed herself some of her own sassafras tea and placed a pen, paper, and inkwell on a crate, which was to serve as her desk. She pulled a kitchen chair over, opened a McGuffey reader, and set the book on end to shield the lantern light from her children. The page showed an upside-down engraving of a boy running with a hoop.

Jennifer sipped her tea from a cup that had been cracked in transit. She checked the two windows, which were black with night. On one sill was the pot of geraniums, which had steadily lost more of their drying petals. A slight breeze, freshened from a light rain, occasionally stirred the sickly flowers. Jennifer turned her attention to her task. She dipped the pen in the inkwell and began to write:

September 7, 1873

Dear Poppa,

Forgive me for not writing to you sooner, but until now I have lived under the illusion that I would not be staying in Kansas long, and that, indeed, I would surely be home as quickly as it would take for a letter to reach you. Alas, that illusion has burst. A commitment I've made—perhaps impetuously—will keep me here until the spring. What that commitment is I will tell you shortly, but there is something else I must tell you first— something very painful.

Please prepare yourself, Poppa, for I know of no gentle way of saying this: Walter has died.

He contracted a fever several days ago. There are no doctors out here, and so a neighbor treated him, this to no avail. He now lies buried in a little cemetery where grasses grow rank among the tombstones. This hurts me. When I think how there will be no one to tend to his grave when I leave Kansas —I wish I could take his body back with me to Ohio, where it may be interred properly beneath some spreading oak.

I miss him, Poppa. He was an exasperating man sometimes, but I did love him. And he loved me— though, on reflection, I can't say why. I was not very supportive of him. I thought only of my own comfort. I never stopped to consider the likelihood that Walter, in coming west, was sacrificing as much as I.

Of course, these are the contrite words of a widow. It is possible—indeed, probable—that if it had been I who died, then it would have been Walter to feel the contrition for dragging me out here.

Oh, Poppa, why couldn't we have stayed in Ohio? I feel like a dandelion seed that has been blown far from home, only to settle on some uncongenial soil. I wish there were no such thing as the West. I wish history had worked out differently, that Thomas Jefferson had never made the Louisiana Purchase. Or I find myself sympathetic to the plight of the local Indians. By all rights, White people shouldn't be here.

Yet I know I don't really care about the Indians. I wish only to let my cowardice appear as something nobler, something righteous. But I will not pretend with you, Poppa. I will tell you outright: I want to come home.

Sometimes I lie awake at night and pretend that is where I am. I needn't even shut my eyes, so dark is it here. Even still, my other senses remind me of the reality, for the prairie wind is always in my ears, and in my own house there is the smell of soil.

Soil? you wonder. That's right, Poppa, for I live in a cave. This is no exaggeration. Walter excavated it for us, displacing a badger in the process.

Do you see now what your daughter has come to? Even as I write, my ceiling—which is little more than the underside of prairie sod—grows damp from rain outside, and the water is seeping into my home. Indeed! Do you see the water mark on this page? It could easily be a tear from me, but it has just fallen from the tangle of roots above my head. And I hear other drops falling upon the floor and furniture in the room. I must pause now, Poppa, and tend to the children . . .

Jennifer put her pen down and lay the McGuffey reader flat so that the lantern's light, though kept on a low flame, filled the room, including the corner where her children slept. The brown floor showed dark dots where the water had struck it. Every so often a glistening drop fell from the mesh of the roots and soil and, with a plop, added another dot to the floor. All the while, outside the two black windows, the rain sizzled.

Careful not to awaken her children, Jennifer arranged a tent of oilskin over them, with one end tucked under their mattress and the other end hanging over the high backs of two chairs. The drops made a louder plop on the tent than they did on the floor.

Jennifer then returned to her crate and saw that several more drops had splotched the page, causing the ink to bleed. The letter was ruined. As she stood there, another drop plopped into the tea cup. Jennifer sighed. She was too tired to start all over. So she abandoned the letter, wrapped herself in oilcloth, and sat on her rocker, where the sound of rain and her own gentle rocking soon put her to sleep.

The next morning, Jennifer awoke to find that her entire floor had turned to mud.

"Momma, look!" said Emma, standing a few feet away, still in her nightgown. "It's up to my ankles!" Peter, meanwhile, walked about, making a sucking sound with his feet in the mud.

Jennifer, still sitting in her rocker and wrapped in the wet oilcloth, gazed at the room, then tossed her head back. "God," she muttered, "give me strength."

All during the rest of that morning, Jennifer and her children lugged all their wet possessions—much of it packed in crates, sacks, and baggage—out of the dugout to dry in the sun. They had help by mid-morning from Joseph Caulder, who rode up on his grey-faced mule. He brought with him a sack of buffalo chips for Jennifer's cookstove and a couple of rabbits he had shot. These things he gave to Jennifer, whereupon he single-handedly hauled out the kitchen table.

Soon, everything was set out in the sun, spread out more than it had been in the dugout. The wet clothing was strewn on the drying grass and hung on a line running from the dugout to the wagon. Tired and perspiring, Jennifer sat in her rocker midst her things, and she looked out onto the prairie.

"It's going to be a hot one," said Joseph, standing before her, looking mostly at the ground. "Your stuff'll be dry before long."

Jennifer arched a seemingly disinterested eyebrow. "And my floor?"

"That'll take longer," said Joseph, kicking mud from his shoes. He looked at the wagon. "I'll grease that axle now."

Overhead, the sky was intensely blue with only a few straggling clouds almost becalmed. Among the furniture flitted an orange-and-black butterfly. "Momma, I'm hungry," said Emma, leaning on the rocker's armrest.

"Please, Emma," snapped Jennifer, "don't hang on me. I'll get you your breakfast. Where's Peter?"

Emma removed herself from the rocker and pointed at her older brother walking at a distance in the grass.

"Tell him not to wander off," said Jennifer, rising from her chair. Emma hurried obediently away. "And put your shoes on!" called Jennifer. She took the sack of buffalo chips and approached her dugout. She considered removing her own shoes to save them from the mud, but she didn't want to be seen barefoot by Joseph Caulder. She sloshed across the mud to the cookstove.

Later, she served breakfast to her children and Joseph at the kitchen table under the big sky. "It's like a picnic!"

declared Emma. She propped up her doll, Melissa, to sit at the table. "Do you want any more flapjacks?" she asked her.

All through breakfast, it was Emma only, conversing with her doll, who enlivened the table. Joseph Caulder, as expected, ate in grim silence, barely looking up from his plate. Peter was still quiet since his father's death. And Jennifer herself had little urge to speak. "Melissa!" said Emma, shaking her head. "I declare, you are being very sloppy."

It was around noon, with Emma playing with a toy tea service, Joseph repairing the ox stalls, and Peter watching him, that Jennifer set out on the cleared kitchen table her inkwell, pen, and a new piece of paper. Once again, she wrote:

Dear Poppa,

But she could go no further. There were too many distractions: a warm breeze kept threatening to blow the page way; a sparrow was perched atop a grass stalk, singing in a high, buzzy voice; the orange-and-black butterfly was still about—or perhaps it was another one—resting on the rocker, its bright wings opening and closing languidly; an occasional bird flew by; and there were the activities of her children and Joseph Caulder.

But what really stole Jennifer's attention was that all-encompassing blue sky. Something so enormous seemed fraught with menace. "There's no telling what'll fall out of a Kansas sky." That's what Bill Wilkes had said.

So, in the short time she had been in Kansas, she had tried learning to read the sky's mood, which was made apparent by its complexion. Sometimes, the sky looked ashen, which meant it might loose a fine all-day rain. Sometimes, it was sickly pale, and that meant a still, muggy day. Sometimes, it was dark and low, and that meant, of course, that something was about to fall out of it with a vengeance, like rain, or that hail.

Then, too, different parts of the sky might be in different

shades, betokening the coming or retreating of storms, or of the sun. Jennifer had come to like dawn and dusk, for that's when the sky showed the rest of its palette: the reds, pinks, and purples.

Jennifer looked up and noted that the last of the straggling clouds had drifted on. The sky now was blue and uninterrupted. Only a lone, distant turkey vulture, a mere speck, marred the dome. It occurred to Jennifer that if she could see the vulture, the vulture could see her, her children, and Joseph: four specks on the prairie.

Yet, in the face of all the enormity, one of those specks, Emma, played with her toy tea service on some flattened grass. "Would you like more muffins?" she asked Melissa, who was sitting on a little chair.

Jennifer watched her daughter, who seemed so much more resilient than Peter about their Poppa's death. Or was it merely some form of blissful innocence? How much more capable did Emma seem than either her brother or her mother to live contentedly in her own imagination. Here she was, after all, in the midst of a grassy wilderness, and yet she played with her make-believe tea service as if she were in the parlor back home.

Jennifer was envious. But then she said to herself, "I can play house, too."

And so, as soon as the mud was dry, Jennifer had everyone move all the possessions back into the dugout. With everything squeezed into place, she stood by the door and thought hard. "You know, I have much red calico," she said as everyone else was getting ready to go outside again. "I could use it to cover these ugly walls."

"Can I help?" asked Emma, growing excited at the project.

"Of course," said Jennifer, sitting herself down at the table to think of other ideas—none of which was likely to make her stay in Kansas enjoyable, but which might at least make it tolerable.

By Monday morning, the first day of school, Jennifer had managed to cover a portion of her dugout walls with different strips of calico, some red and some blue. The dugout seemed so much improved by these modest decorations that, while not especially proud, Jennifer was not ashamed to receive her neighbors' children.

There were, including Peter and Emma, seventeen children in her newly bedecked dugout that morning. The youngest among them—Mary Baker—was six years old, and the oldest, as it happened, was Todd Baker, who was sixteen. Some of the children had arrived by horse, but most had walked, covering many miles.

As they all crowded into the cramped, murky room, each student approached Jennifer with a gift—or rather her payment—before finding some spot to sit or stand. "My maw said to give you this oil," grumbled Todd, presenting a small tin before shuffling off into a corner to join his brother and sister, clearly annoyed at having to be inside on such a sunny day.

"Here's cornbread for you, Mrs. Vandermeer," said a little, dark-skinned, black girl, holding the unwrapped loaf in one hand and her younger brother's hand in the other.

"My mother baked this chicken pie for you," said one of two red-haired twin boys, the other grabbing a chair from a girl at the table.

"My pa said he'll bring you some flour when he gets the wheat milled," said a little blonde girl in pigtails.

"My fotter und mutter vant me to invite you to dinner," said a sandy-haired boy.

Jennifer accepted all these items graciously and placed them where she could among the dugout's clutter. With her students settled down, she took a moment to note them all. Some, like the twin boys, their red hair slicked back, were dressed in their Sunday best. Most, however, were in patched-together clothing and barefoot. She was surprisingly calm standing before them all. Except for some whispering, and for one boy tugging at the pigtails of the blonde girl, the children were well-behaved. Perhaps their parents had threatened to whump them if they weren't, or perhaps they were slightly awed at being in a schoolhouse, even one as humble as this. Only one boy made Jennifer nervous. He was a dark, beady-eyed child who stood at the rear of the room and rocked from side to side, grunting every so often. The other children didn't seem to mind him.

"I think," started Jennifer—but she had to stop to clear her throat. "I think we ought to begin by introducing ourselves. As most of you already know, my name is Mrs. Vandermeer." Jennifer paused. "Um, now why don't each of you tell us your name—and where you're from?"

Each student took a turn telling the class his or her name, and where he or she came from. The blonde girl with the pigtails was named Clara Anderson, and she was from Illinois; the dark-skinned black girl was named Laura Franklin, her brother, Jonathan, and her family was from a Virginia plantation; the twin boys were Michael and James McCormick, and they were from Boston and, before that, Ireland; the sandy-haired boy was Rolf Meyer, and he was from Bavaria; and so on and so forth. Only two children didn't do as they were asked: the beady-eyed boy, whose name was Jeffrey Hodge, wasn't sure what state his parents came from; and Peter, who, still so sad, refused to speak.

Jennifer was angry with her uncooperative son, but she didn't push the issue. There was a more pressing problem. So involved had she been in sprucing up her dugout that she hadn't given much thought to how she was going to conduct her class. And Lucy had not come up with a blackboard. It was only now that Jennifer realized what a handicap that was going to be. Indeed, for a painfully long second or two, she wasn't sure how she was to continue. But then she saw her broom leaning against the wall, and she took it. "Our first lesson will be in Geography."

The room fell silent, except for someone's loud and resigned groan.

Jennifer positioned herself by the door where there was some space, and, using the broom's handle, she began to etch something in the dirt. All the children leaned forward to see. "These are the states between Kansas and Ohio," said Jennifer.

"Where's Ireland?" asked one of the McCormick twins.

"We won't concern ourselves with that today," said Jennifer.

When she had exhausted what she knew about the region under discussion, Jennifer turned the broom around and erased the map. It was all awkward, this teaching business, and Jennifer wasn't sure she was going about it quite right. The time seemed to pass very slowly. According to the mantel clock sitting on the bureau only fifteen minutes had gone by, and already she had nothing further to say about Geography. So she turned to ciphering, writing the numbers on the floor with the broom handle. But the students became bored and restless after so many minutes. The beady-eyed boy, Jeffrey, groaned loudly and began rocking more violently.

How long was she supposed to hold class anyway? And even if she did keep the students busy for several hours, they would be back the next day! Then the day after! And the day after that! And on and on!...

Jennifer spent the rest of the morning using the McGuffey readers. She had only seven copies, and some were in bad condition, being a couple of decades old. But they were more useful than the Bibles some students had brought, since there were too many versions of the Word, a couple being in German.

When, at last, by morning's end, Jennifer had taught all she had to teach, she dismissed her students. They slammed their books closed and, squealing, pushing, and teasing each other, they burst forth from the dugout like seeds of a ripe pod.

"Come back next Monday!" called Jennifer as they dispersed across the tall grass. She needed time to better plan her next class.

Emma, meanwhile, waved good-bye to the boys and girls, delighted at having had so many children visit her in her home. "Bye, Mary! Bye, Rolf! Bye Jeremy! . . ."

As the children heard their names, they each turned and waved back, even the beady-eyed boy, who tried to return her call: "Bah, Emma!"

Peter, however, had no part in this. Instead, he walked off alone into the grass and sat down, vanishing.

Jennifer almost got angry at him again, but she quickly saddened. It broke her heart to see him in class with all the other children, most of whom—including Emma—seemed impatient for class to end just so they could talk and play together. Peter barely acknowledged them. He just stood in his corner, his distant blue eyes avoiding contact with those around him. If another child whispered something in his ear, he turned his head away.

That night, after dinner, Jennifer said to him, "Peter, I miss Poppa too, but at least I'm talking."

Peter didn't answer. He sat in a corner and sullenly pretended to be reading one of the books.

"You know, the other children will start to make fun of you if you're not friendlier."

Peter remained tight-jawed. He stared blankly at the pages before him, and only the heavy rise and fall of his chest indicated that some upsetting thought was floating through his young mind.

"Is there nothing I can do to make you feel better?" asked Jennifer, standing several feet away on the ciphers still etched into the floor.

Peter's resolute mouth began to tremble, but he said nothing.

Jennifer took a step toward her son. She prayed he might run into her arms. She wanted so badly to hold him. But he was a stubborn little boy. Indeed, reflected Jennifer, he was perhaps being as stubbornly silent as she herself had been on the journey out there.

"You know, you're making me and Emma sad," said Jennifer. "Is that what you want?"

Peter flipped a page. His eyes didn't even follow it.

"See here, young man," tried Jennifer more sternly, her hands resting on her hips, "I will not put up with this silence in my house! While you are living under my roof, you must . . ."

But she couldn't finish her sentence. She saw such unhappiness and pain upon the face of her son that she felt her throat tighten and tears well up in her eyes. Without another word, she turned and hurried outside so her children wouldn't see her cry, and she walked up the rise to the rear of the dugout so that they would not hear her, either. When, upon looking back, she could barely see the stove pipe in the ground, she went no farther, and she tossed herself onto the grass. There she curled like a doe on the ground that radiated from her to that great encircling horizon. The darkened blue dome reigned overhead, its western edge tinted with the pastel colors of a half-submerged sun painting the underside of some clouds. Jennifer buried her head and sobbed, her plaintive call mixing with the evening chirping of crickets and the staccato call of dickcissals. "I taught him well . . ."

Finally, her tears slowing, Jennifer raised her head to look back at the stove pipe for reassurance. But what she saw, stretched out across the sunset-reddened grass, was the enlongated shadow of a person. She turned quickly and squinted into the setting sun's oncoming rays, which were eclipsed by the silhouette of a man wearing a broad-brimmed hat and great, bushy side-whiskers.

Chapter Eight
An Unpopular Woman

"Hello, Mrs. Vandermeer." A sonorous voice came from the silhouette.

Jennifer raised one hand to shield out the sun, and she could just make out the mutton-chopped visage of Bill Wilkes. He stooped down so that their faces were close. His form still blocked part of the sun, so that a halo formed around him.

"Is something the matter?" he asked.

Jennifer began to raise herself from the ground, and Wilkes helped her to her feet. "Excuse me," said Jennifer, embarrassed. "It's been a difficult day."

"You know, you ought to be careful at this hour. The rattlers become active at dusk." Jennifer quickly scanned the grass around her. "Come on," said Wilkes, "let's head back to your dugout." He offered Jennifer his arm. He patted Jennifer's hand. "I thought I lost you there a moment. I saw you run up here while I was still on the trail, but when I got here, you were nowhere in sight—until I nearly tripped over you."

The two came to the stove pipe and stopped. Feeling somewhat reassured by the tall, handsome man, Jennifer turned to watch the last wisps of color on the western horizon get quenched by the deepening night. "You know, back home, I never noticed the sunsets. I must say, they are pretty.''

Wilkes, his hold on Jennifer's arm weakened by her turn, released her. ''Well, I reckon you have sunsets enough back in Ohio.''

Jennifer laughed. ''I suppose we do—my, you do tend to catch me when I'm indisposed. The last time, my husband was afraid you'd find a good joke in my refusing to leave the wagon.''

''No, you were unhappy. That's understandable.'' Wilkes stepped closer to Jennifer, trying to steal her attention from the sunset. ''A lady of your obvious refinement is best suited for the East.''

Jennifer turned to Wilkes—his face, whiskers and all, were growing faint in the darkness—and she smiled. ''You're kind to say so.''

''I mean it. Leave this prairie for those people better off in it—people who have little stake in the east, who have little to lose by coming out here.''

''That's exactly the way I feel, Mr. Wilkes.''

''Really? Well, I heard you were planning to stay—that you'd be teaching school here, or some such nonsense.''

Jennifer tightened. She clasped her arms. ''I do believe the evenings are getting chillier,'' she said, glassy-eyed.

''Mrs. Vandermeer, I'll be frank with you. This isn't entirely a social visit. As land agent, I'm obliged to find out if you plan on staying on your property. Other folks can use it if you're not going to.''

''Really, Mr. Wilkes, there's so much land around. Surely I'm not depriving anyone.''

Wilkes stroked his whiskers thoughtfully. ''Can we go inside, Mrs. Vandermeer? It'd be easier to talk.''

''Certainly. I didn't mean to be inhospitable.'' Jennifer stepped toward the decline. She held up the hem of her skirt with one hand, and held onto Wilkes' hand with the other.

She and he stepped down to where Wilkes' bay was tied before the dugout. They went in.

The room was already dully lit from an oil lamp, but Peter had gone to bed, leaving Emma up alone. Emma ran up to her mother and hugged her skirt. "Peter wouldn't stay up," she complained, her eyes teary. "I was afraid."

Jennifer sighed, eyeing her sleeping son curled up in the corner on the mattress. She patted her daughter's head. "There's nothing to be afraid of. I was just outside." She turned to Wilkes. "Please do sit. I'll make us some tea." She then stooped and addressed Emma. "Now it's your turn to go to bed. It's late."

Emma turned to her doll sitting on the rocker. "I told you not to be afraid," she said. Whereupon she walked obediently off to dress for bed.

Jennifer straightened and walked over to the cookstove.

"Mrs. Vandermeer, please don't trouble yourself," said Wilkes. "I'm not much of a tea drinker." He gestured for Jennifer to sit at the table.

She did so, across from him, her hands folded.

"Now about this school business," said Wilkes.

"I do have coffee, if you'd prefer."

"No, thanks. Mrs. Vandermeer, do you really want to teach out here?"

Jennifer fell silent.

"I didn't think so. Whose idea was it, anyway?"

"Lucy Baker thought . . . "

"Ah! Lucy. I should have known. No disrepect to her, but sometimes that woman can't mind her own business. Her head's filled with ideas about what she'd like to see out here, but your obligation is to yourself, not to Lucy Baker."

"But I can't go back on my word. I already agreed to stay until the spring. Lucy said a railroad spur might be in town by then—and by your efforts."

"Yeah, but by the spring? She knows very well it won't

be done so quickly. You can't always listen to what Lucy says. Now, between you and me . . . "

Just then, Emma, dressed in her nightgown and carrying her doll, returned to Jennifer to say good night. Jennifer kissed her and kissed Melissa too. "Say good night to Mr. Wilkes," she instructed.

Emma faced the shaggy-faced guest. "Good night."

" 'Night," responded Wilkes abruptly.

Emma hurried over to the mattress with a quick pat on her rump from her mother.

"Mrs. Vandermeer, as I was saying, this railroad, you just can't wait for it . . . "

"Shh," went Jennifer, raising a finger to her lips.

"You just can't wait for it," repeated Wilkes more softly, but excitedly. "To tell you the truth, I don't know if it'll ever come. There are too many farms springing up around the town."

"Why, I'd have thought that could only help."

"No, the Kansas Pacific likes to hook up with cattle trails. That's where the money is—shipping Texas cattle. The farms out here are starting to cut off Four Corners from the trails." Wilkes, who had been growing increasingly agitated, calmed himself. "The point is, if I were you, I wouldn't wait for any railroad."

"Well, unfortunately, I can't return east without one."

"Hell, I'll take you to a rail town if that's what's stopping you."

"But I promised Lucy . . . "

"To hell with that woman!"

"Your voice, Mr. Wilkes . . . "

Wilkes rose suddenly from his chair. "To hell with my voice!" he snapped. "Look, Mrs. Vandermeer, you're already mostly packed, so let's cut the nonsense. I'm going to assume you'll do the smart thing." He stepped over to the door and opened it. He put his hat on. "After all, you have your children to think of. So let me know soon, and I'll escort you to a railtown. Good night.'' He left, slamming the door.

Jennifer remained sitting and listened as Wilkes rode off.

"Momma, I'm glad he left,'' called Emma from the mattress.

Jennifer turned. "Shush. Go to sleep.''

"He's a bully, right, Momma?''

Jennifer returned her gaze to the door and windows. "He's trying to be.''

The next morning, Jennifer, for the first time, awaited Joseph Caulder's arrival eagerly. She wanted to tell him about Wilkes's visit. She now remembered all too clearly that Wilkes had been the topic of conversation at Lucy's house. Her neighbors apparently didn't like the man, and she was sure Joseph would be most interested to know what Wilkes's business was at her place. When Jennifer at last espied Joseph riding up the trail on his mule, she actually felt relieved, and she hurried to prepare him some coffee.

Only it wasn't Joseph. It was his brother, Isaac.

"That's curious,'' said Jennifer, stepping forward from her doorway.

As he pulled off the trail and onto the property, Isaac, as straight-faced as his brother, nodded at Jennifer, who responded in kind. She waited patiently as the mule trudged over to her dugout. She noted for the first time how much older Isaac was than his brother. He seemed almost old enough to be Joseph's father. Or had the prairie simply taken a greater toll on him?

"Good morning, Mr. Caulder,'' said Jennifer, daring to smile.

Isaac Caulder nodded quickly once more. "Mrs. Vandermeer,'' he said. He stayed atop his mule.

"Is there something I can do for you?'' asked Jennifer,

shading her eyes with one hand. "I was expecting Joseph."

Isaac seemed even more shy than his brother, and he turned his head away, preferring to look at the ground as he spoke. "I'd like a word with you."

"Why, certainly," said Jennifer. "Why don't you come in?"

"I'd as soon as not. This won't take long."

Jennifer lifted a curious eyebrow. "Is something the matter?"

"Nothing that can't be fixed." Isaac now looked off in the distance. "I just wanted you to know my brother won't be coming around here anymore."

"Won't he?"

"He's got enough work on our own place."

"I thought he might. Frankly, I was wondering where he found the time to come here. Not that I didn't appreciate his help. He's a very generous man."

"Maybe too generous." Isaac looked to the ground again. "And—I'd appreciate it if you wouldn't lead him on so."

At this, Jennifer, her mouth agape, stepped back. "Lead him? . . ."

"The Lord sees all, ma'am. You oughtn't take advantage of a man because you think he's lonely."

"Mr. Caulder!"

"Now, I won't argue with you. Just leave my brother be."

Jennifer became so flustered she could hardly speak. She stepped right back up to the mule. "You are making very improper suggestions!"

"I'm being direct, ma'am. As direct as I can be. I don't have anyone else to help me, and I can't afford to have my brother go running off and making a fool of himself over some woman. The least you could have done was pay him for his work."

Jennifer stood there, glaring at the grim man. "Now you listen to me," she started. "First of all, it was not my idea that your brother come over here. I told him repeatedly that he should tend to his own farm first. Second of all, I resent your coming onto my property and making insinuations about my righteousness, as if it were your business. And finally, what right do you have to make such decisions for your brother? He's forty-two and old enough, I think, to decide these things for himself.''

"My brother, ma'am, is a fool over some matters and would likely commit blasphemy if I didn't watch over him.''

Jennifer nearly sputtered in frustration, but she spoke slowly, "I wish to say only one last thing, Mr. Caulder. And that is, you are mistaken about me.''

Isaac Caulder nodded curtly as if to say her comment was as good a way as any to end the conversation, whereupon he pulled his mule about and started back toward the trail.

As she watched her neighbor ride off, Jennifer tried to calm herself. She slowly did. Remembering Wilkes' visit, she thought, almost amused, My, how unpopular I've suddenly become.

So many thoughts now entered Jennifer's head that she could barely sort them out. She was surprised to realize that she might actually miss Joseph puttering grimly about her property. And while she resented Isaac for his forwardness, she also felt sorry for him. He seemed a lonely man and was perhaps frightened of losing his brother.

For Wilkes, however, Jennifer had no sympathy. How two-faced he had shown himself to be! He would never have tried to push Walter around. But Walter's wife? That was another story!

Jennifer was only getting herself riled thinking of Wilkes, and she decided it was best to occupy her mind with matters more pleasant or, at least, more pressing. She decided to plan her next class. This worked, but only so far. Even as she sat at her table, Jennifer couldn't help but stay her pen to think of that so-called land agent. The coward! The bully! Indeed, so preoccupied with him had she really become, whether she cared to admit it or not, that he even entered, that very night, her dream.

In it, Jennifer stood before her class. Among the many youthful faces of her students was added one more—the bewhiskered Wilkes. He was well enough behaved, but he was standing in the back of the room and rocking from side to side, just like the dark-eyed boy. Jennifer was wary of him. Then, one of her students said, "Look at the pretty sunrise, Momma." Sunrise? During class? Have we started so early today?

Jennifer began to awaken. Her eyelids drew back like two tiny stage curtains, preparing her for the next act in some interminable opera. Strangely, the room was cast in a faint, flickering light. Jennifer sat up. Emma was standing several feet away, gazing out one window at a distant glow emanating along the length of the horizon.

"But the sun doesn't rise there," said Jennifer, still half in her dream. She slid out of bed and threw her robe and slippers on. She joined Emma and watched the glow, too.

"Isn't it pretty, Momma?"

All along the horizon was a thin fringe of shimmering light. In the sky overhead were great billowing dark clouds, their undersides luridly illuminated.

"Oh, God," gasped Jennifer in sudden realization. "It's coming this way!"

Chapter Nine
Annealed With Heat

"Quick! Find Poppa's scythe!" cried Jennifer, looking about the room.

"What's a scythe?" asked Emma, searching fervently.

Peter, barefoot and dressed in his nightgown, approached his mother with the long-handled tool. Jennifer grabbed it and hurried outside. "Don't leave the dugout!"

She started whacking away at the trampled grass before her home.

The fringe of light, meanwhile, had grown thicker, nearer, and its billowing smoke was being born ahead of it by high winds, so that the stars over the dugout were disappearing behind an encroaching, inky shroud. Ashes and flakes began to rain down on Jennifer's head, as if the benighted dome itself were crumbling. Every so often, a rabbit broke forth into the clearing, fleeing the approaching light fringe.

Jennifer had now shorn away a broad swath in front of her home. As she began to gather the cut grass in her arms to dump beyond the clearing, a pall of black smoke drifted past her, smarting her eyes and making her cough.

"Stay inside, I said!" she shouted, noticing her children in the open doorway.

"It's a fire, Momma!" shouted Emma.

Peter hurried outside and began to help his mother gather the cut grass. Emma followed.

"Keep back!" cried Jennifer frantically as she stooped to gather more grass. A prairie chicken hurried past her. Then a couple of deer bounded across the small clearing. Birds skimmed overhead. The oxen in their stalls lowed fretfully. "Stay inside!"

Peter and Emma continued to gather the grass and dump it away from the dugout.

The fire was closer still. Everyone and everything around the dugout was lit up. Jennifer heard the dull roar of incinerating grass. She felt the first wave of heat. The four bellowing oxen, in a panic, broke free of the posts that secured them, and they burst forth from the hay-covered structure to join the wild animals in flight.

"All right! Inside!" shouted Jennifer, ushering her children back into the dugout. She slammed the door behind her. The room bore a dark haze.

"Will we burn up?" asked Emma.

"No, our home is made of earth," answered Jennifer, her chest heaving. She looked out the paneless windows at the fast-appproaching wall of flame, which poured swelling black smoke, balls of torched grass, and sparks into the sky. So wide was this wall, which soared forty feet high, that Jennifer couldn't see its ends. And so near was it that the room was filled with its roar, light, and ever more of its heat.

"I'm scared," said Emma, clinging to her mother's robe. "I want Poppa!"

Peter backed up to the deepest recess of the dugout. His blue eyes wide with fright, he stared at the brightly lit windows that framed the holocaust outside. At his feet were two rabbits, a prairie chicken, some field mice, and other critters that had stumbled into the dugout when the door was open. He was joined by his mother and sister, who retreated from the gaping windows and searing heat. Jennifer prayed it would get no hotter.

But it did. Hesitating only briefly at Joseph's fire-break,

the fire leapt over and roared on toward the dugout faster than a man could run. Its heat turned the soddy into an oven. Thick smoke streamed in through the two windows, making Jennifer and her children choke and their eyes tear. Jennifer started for the windows to close the shutters, but the smoke overwhelmed her, and she forced her children onto the dirt floor and held them tightly under her. The roar became deafening; the light, blinding; the heat, scorching. "Oh, God . . . ''

Then, suddenly, a portion of the fiery palisade sputtered as it moved across the clearing Jennifer had made. It was in this enfeebled state that the flames approached the last few yards to her dugout, sparing those inside the brunt of its heat. The flames passed as if on tiptoe, only to streak up the rise into which the dugout was built and swell again on the roof, where unshorn grasses remained.

Inside, the room was plunged back into darkness. The roar grew fainter. The windows now framed only the residue of the departed blaze: patches of fire and bursts of sparks, the pot of withered geraniums, but mostly there was black night.

With the coming of the true sunrise some hours later, the prairie was revealed as blackened and dead. Some fires still smoldered, and smoke rose from the ground here and there. The air smelled acrid. There was no longer the hum of insects or the chirping of birds. There was only the wind.

"Momma, it all looks so different," commented Emma, standing barefoot in her nightgown and gawking at the blackened scene from the open door.

Peter, also barefoot and in his bedclothes, stepped outside but quickly retreated, for the ground was hot.

"Go dress," said Jennifer, clutching her own robe closed. She scanned the transformed landscape. Everything within the horizon was crisped. The prairie trail appeared no longer as a rent in the lush grass, but as a faint stripe.

As she let her eyes follow that stripe into the distance, Jennifer saw, just coming over the northern horizon, a rider atop what appeared to be an ungainly running mule. He'll be here soon, thought Jennifer. She hurried to dress, scooting outside a lingering rabbit.

Jennifer had just finished tucking her blouse into her skirt when the man rode up.

"Why, Joseph," said Jennifer, stepping from her doorway, "I didn't expect to see you again."

For the first time that Jennifer had known him, Joseph was agitated and trying to catch his breath. There was an urgency in his usual slow, deep voice. "You're all right?" he asked, looking at her with his dark, intense eyes in unaccustomed boldness.

"We're fine," said Jennifer. "As you can see."

Joseph noted everyone, and this seemed to take steam out of him. He calmed down. Already at a loss for more words, he looked off some dozen yards and gestured with his head. "Plow's burnt."

Lying on the barren ground was what remained of the plow, a curved metal blade, partly melted and attached to some charred wood.

"My wagon, too," added Jennifer, pointing to the collapsed heap. "And my oxen have run off!"

"Guess I didn't make that fire-break wide enough," said Joseph.

"Now don't go blaming yourself for anything," said Jennifer. "At least I had no crops to lose. How did you fare?"

Joseph, ever returning to his familiar ways, squinted off in the distance. His breathing had grown steadier, his voice quieter. "We were north of the fire."

"You were fortunate," said Jennifer. She watched Joseph as he apparently struggled to make conversation. But there was only an awkward second or two of silence. "And the town?"

"Wasn't touched," But even as Joseph answered, his attention was already diverted by something to the south. "Damn," he muttered.

Jennifer turned to see. Riding up the trail was a buggy. "It looks like Karl," she said.

"Looks it," said Joseph, his face darkening.

When Karl Pfeffer arrived, he jumped off his buggy with surprising agility for a man of his age and weight. He hurried to take Jennifer by the hands. "Dear Mrs. Vandermeer—Jenny—I am zo glad you are zafe und zound!"

"Thank you, Karl. And your family?"

"Dey are fine, but ve lost zo much vheat."

"Oh, I'm so sorry."

"Ve vill get by, I guess. Hello, Jozeph."

Joseph nodded curtly. "Karl."

Jennifer shuddered. "I've never seen anything like it."

"Ach! Dat Vilkes," muttered Karl.

"Wilkes?" came back Jennifer, discretely removing her hands from Karl's.

"Ya, ya, I vouldn't be surpised!"

"You're not suggesting . . ."

"He vants us out of here!"

"Yes, but to set a fire?"

Joseph, meanwhile, feeling left out, cleared his throat loudly. "You know, Jennifer, I can loan you a mule."

Jennifer, duly distracted, turned her attention to Joseph.

"You'll need something to ride on," he explained.

"Why, yes, you're right. Thank you."

"Ach! A mule!" returned Karl quickly, throwing his shoulders back. "I vill loan you a horse!"

"I already offered," said Joseph sternly.

"Come now, Jozeph, you expect a lady to ride a mule?"

"Nothing wrong with that."

"Gentlemen," said Jennifer, "please let's not argue over such matters."

"Jenny, you vait," said Karl, hurrying to his buggy. "I

vill bring you a goot mare.''

"I'll bring that mule," said Joseph, pulling himself up onto his own grey-muzzled animal.

"Really, both of you!''

"I vill be back,'' said Karl, flicking his reins.

"Me, too,'' said Joseph, spurring his mule, which complained nasally at the kick.

And the two men rode off in separate directions. Jennifer shook her head. For all the blackened devastation before her, she couldn't help but smile.

Later that afternoon, Joseph and Karl returned at almost the same time. Karl rode up first on his Studebaker buggy, followed by a buckboard driven by a blonde young man of around twenty, apparently his son. Joseph, meanwhile, was approaching on his mule, with a second, saddled mule in tow.

Karl stopped before the dugout. Jennifer approached, but before she could say anthing, Karl stood up in his buggy and called out, "Jozeph! I told you not to bodder!''

"Please don't start with him," said Jennifer, a hand resting on a front wheel of the buggy.

Joseph, riding onto Jennifer's property, didn't answer but waited until he got close enough. Then he said, "And I thought I told you.''

"How can you expect a lady to ride dat stupid beast!''

"This 'stupid beast', I reckon, is a better mount than any nag of yours.''

"Vell, I am giffing her alzo dis buggy!''

This caught Joseph off guard. "Yeah, well, I got a wagon I can loan her.''

Placing herself between the two men—Karl still standing in his buggy and Joseph slumped-shouldered atop his mule— Jennifer raised her hands in a bid for peace. "Gentlemen! I appreciate both your offers!''

"Jozeph, you are putting her in an awkward pozition!''

"You are!''

"You both are!" shouted Jennifer, finally silencing the two men. She took a breath. "I tell you what. I can borrow Karl's buggy and hitch it to Joseph's mule. How does that sound?"

"Ach! Do you zee the complications you are causing, Jozeph?" asked Karl.

"Ain't nothing complicated about it," replied Joseph, grateful he was not to be outdone by his competitor.

"You are zuch a baby," grumbled Karl, shaking his head as he stepped down to unhitch his horse from the buggy. Joseph, meanwhile, dismounted to remove the saddle from the rear mule.

As she waited, Jennifer finally had a moment to acknowledge Karl's son, who was either shy or a bit embarrassed by his father's display, for he shifted uncomfortably on the buckboard seat. "Good afternoon," said Jennifer.

"Afternoon, ma'am," he replied with an uneasy smile.

The two men practically had a tug-of-war to see who would harness the mule to the buggy.

And, while they fought, yet another rider, this one atop a black horse, appeared approaching the soddy. For a moment, Jennifer thought it might be Wilkes. That would be good timing, she thought, what with Karl and Joseph present—and in a combative mood.

But it wasn't Wilkes. It was Todd Baker. He rode up, nodded at Karl's son, then addressed Jennifer, trying to speak over the arguing of the two men harnessing the mule. "Afternoon, Mrs. Vandermeer."

"Todd," responded Jennifer, plugging one ear against the yelling.

"My maw sent me to see if you're all right."

"That's very nice of her. Tell her we are all fine. How did your family do?"

"Fire didn't touch us."

"How fortunate."

"Hi, Todd," came in Emma, running up to the horse.
Todd nodded abruptly at the little girl.

". . . Jozeph, you are in der vay!"

"No, you are! . . ."

"And the Camps?" continued Jennifer. "How did they fare?"

"Not so good," said Todd. "Lost their crops. They're talking of leaving."

Jennifer started. She squinted at Todd and stepped closer to him to hear better. "What was that? Leaving?"

"That's what they said."

". . . Jozeph, you are hopeless!"

"You are . . . !"

"You mean for good?" asked Jennifer, stepping still closer.

"Yep. My maw's real mad with them."

Jennifer couldn't believe what she was hearing. Wasn't it Nancy who begged her not to return to Ohio? What right did this woman now have to leave? "Surely you heard wrong."

Todd only shrugged.

". . . Jozeph, I am telling fur der last time!"

"No, I'm telling you!"

"Ach . . . !"

Two days passed. With the black land reddened by an early morning sun, a small covered wagon, drawn by four horses, stopped on the trail beside Jennifer's property. Throwing a shawl around her shoulders, Jennifer left her children to finish their breakfast and hurried to the wagon. Sitting up front were Will and Nancy Camp. Jennifer couldn't believe her eyes—couldn't believe Nancy's audacity. "So you are leaving," she said simply. Wisps of her dark hair blew in the light wind.

Will, his Adam's apple rising and falling as he swallowed hard, turned his head away and squinted off in the distance.

"Yes," said Nancy defensively, adjusting her bonnet.

"The fire, you know. It destroyed everything. Will must find work elsewhere."

"But you will be coming back."

"No, I'm afraid not. We've—had enough."

"I'm sorry to hear this," said Jennifer coolly.

"So was Lucy," said Nancy, slipping her arm around her husband's and hugging it tightly. "She became downright abusive to us."

"Did she?"

"No surprise. But this time we told her our minds were made up!"

Are they? thought Jennifer. And are you the only ones allowed to make up your minds?

"I guess we're just not made as sturdily as her," continued Nancy, "Or you, for that matter."

This caught Jennifer by surprise. She was flattered to be thought of as "sturdy" for once, though she felt dishonest about it. She had fooled someone—someone perhaps even weaker than she. And maybe that's all anyone ever really did. Maybe, even, she herself had been fooled all along by her husband, her father, Lucy, and everyone else.

"So we've come to say good-bye," said Nancy, her voice lowering in sadness. "I didn't want you to think too ill of me."

"Won't you stay a while?" asked Jennifer, feeling more benevolent.

"We've waited too long as it is," came in Will. "It's getting late in the season. I don't want to be caught in an early blizzard."

Nancy turned to him. "Surely another hour won't make a difference?"

"We've got to be going," said Will, reluctant to take his eyes off the southern horizon.

"Are—you returning to Maryland?" asked Jennifer.

"Texas," said Nancy. "Will's going to try finding work

on a ranch. He's worked with horses before.''

"I see," said Jennifer, her eyes growing distant. "Well, then I guess I should wish you luck.''

"Thank you," said Will. "And good luck to you.'' He flicked the reins. His horses started up.

"We'll write to you when we settle in," called Nancy as the little wagon rattled on.

"Please do!" returned Jennifer, taking a step or two with the wagon. Her throat tightened.

"Maybe you can visit us one day!" called Nancy, turning in her seat to look back as the wagon pulled ahead.

"Maybe I will!''

"We must stay friends!" cried Nancy, her voice becoming fainter in the growing distance.

"We will!" Jennifer waved. She could no longer make out what Nancy was shouting. She waved once more and watched the wagon until it was very small in the distance.

She suddenly felt very lonely. Before even the wagon could disappear over the horizon, she hurried into her dugout. She sat herself at her writing crate, unscrewed the inkwell, and took up her pen.

October 9, 1873

Dear Poppa,

I can only imagine how worried you must be not having heard from me sooner. This letter is actually my second attempt. And I suspect it will be rather different from the one I had originally intended, so much has happened to me since then.

But first I have a painful duty to perform. I have sad news, so please prepare yourself. Walter has passed away. He died of a fever last summer.

My heart is with you, Poppa. I know how close you and Walter were. I wish I could be with you now so that we might comfort each other. But you may take solace, at least, in knowing that your daughter and grandchildren are doing well.

That in itself is a remarkable thing. Since coming west, I have suffered every imaginable tribulation. Each time, I thought surely I would not last. And yet, here I sit, in the quiet ccol of an autumn afternoon, writing you this letter.

One never knows the trials, even the worst, that can be endured until one is tested. We have resources deep within us that need rarely be tapped, that, indeed, lay dormant and unseen. But I have been forced to draw upon those resources—or should I say they rose to the surface of their own accord, when needed, ever surprising me.

Like metal that is subjected to repeated heat and cold, I feel my spirit annealed. Yet, I add, this would not have been the case had I not paused to reflect upon my survival, for it is in this very act of reflection that we may bestow upon ourselves the strength I speak of. That is the trick. That is what I have learned out here. I have seen others suffer as much as I and not realize that they were my equals as survivors. They granted me that which they themselves possessed, if only they stopped to see it.

I have. And I will try not to forget it. Even as I emerge from a prairie inferno, I am about to be plunged into a prairie winter. Talk of annealing! I am sure you do not believe that these are the words of the daughter who sat with you in the parlor for so many years. And, indeed, I confess there remains a part of me that is as frightened as ever, that wishes only to go home and be your little girl again. But this, too, I accept. And, come the spring, I will not fight it. Be patient, Poppa. You will find me returned home with the first robins in our yard.

*Now you must forgive the brevity of this letter, but
I am intent on mailing it. Lord knows when it will
actually leave the town. I promise to write again, and
at greater length soon. And so, until we are reunited,
I send you all my love, and all the children's love.*

Ever your daughter,
Jenny

*P.S. I will be staying with a neighboring family this
winter, so do not fear for me.*

The ink was barely dry when Jennifer sealed up the letter and rode into town to leave it at Pearson's Inn. There it was put in a sack with letters from her neighbors, some of which were already a month old, awaiting travelers passing through town, in any direction, to take them away.

Meanwhile, the season was slowly beginning to change. Before long, her students were leaving to help their families with the harvesting. Every day, it seemed the wind blew just a bit cooler and harder. Soon, wriggling skeins of geese appeared in the sky, honking their way south. The noon sun no longer reached so high, nor the days lasted so long.

Then Lucy said it was time. Jennifer and her children loaded up the buggy and rode to the Baker homestead. And there they stayed as the wind turned still colder, the days shorter, and as, at last, the first dusting of snow settled on the soddy's roof, the solitary elm, the harvested field, and, like a poultice, the burnt prairie.

Chapter Ten
...and Cold

Early in the season those first snows continued to fall only lightly. Whatever lay on the ground was either melted away by the noon sun or blown away by the wind.

But, before long, the winter began in earnest, and snow flaked off the great grey dome almost unceasingly, so that the ground was covered in white and stayed that way. Sometimes the snow fell straight down, but, more often, it fell in lashing winds. Only occasionally did the winter take a breath, when the sky blushed blue, and critters punched out of the snow from their buried burrows to forage.

Then everyone in the Baker soddy likewise hurried outside to get some elbow room. The children rolled around, threw snowballs, dug tunnels, built snowmen, and took turns sledding down the embankment formed on the lee side of the soddy. During some weeks, it was possible to go out nearly every day, which the adults appreciated as much as the children. Nothing was more refreshing than to step outside in the morning, feel the slap of cold on the cheek, and see the brilliant white landscape sprawling in every direction to meet the deep blue sky at the horizon. The clear, brisk air seemed to crystalize everything and sharpened even the most distant objects.

But always the sky eventually darkened, and the snows returned, layering the prairie with an even thicker, seamless white blanket. Then, each morning, with shovels in hands, Seth and the boys sallied forth from the soddy to make sure there were clear paths to the stable, well, and outhouse. As the winter wore on, these paths became ever more deeply etched in the rising snow so that the shovelers had to heft the snow higher and higher to clear the way.

When there was no digging to do, Seth and the boys tried to occupy themselves with other endeavors, like making bullets, waterproofing their boots with hog lard, sharpening tools for the spring, or, when weather permitted, hunting. Once, Seth dashed breathlessly into the soddy. "Buffalo!" he shouted as he tied on his snowshoes. Everyone crowded through the door to see—half way to the horizon was a small herd of buffalo, trudging in four, long, brown files through haunch-high snow. Seth grabbed his rifle and hurried after them. Unfortuately, the buffalo were moving away from the soddy and Seth couldn't get close enough for a good shot. He gave it a try, but the rifle report only scared the animals into running, plowing the snow before them. Seth watched them move off, his rifle dangling at his side, his chest heaving. Everyone was disappointed as they watched him return, but Lucy said, "It was not meant to be."

When, by and by, they couldn't find work for themselves, or when the weather forbade them from leaving the soddy, Seth and the boys were impressed into woman's work. "There's no sense being idle," said Lucy. "If you want to eat tonight, you must help with the cooking."

"It happens every winter," explained Seth to Peter, his hand on the boy's shoulder. "I can put it off only so long."

Peter smiled and gave a quick shrug. It lifted Jennifer's heart to see her son behave so congenially, and she was grateful to Seth. She thought, He's being a father to Peter. He's a good man.

Indeed, at times, Jennifer found herself a little jealous of Lucy for having such a good husband. He seemed so even-tempered—yet so strong—and surprisingly talented! Sometimes, in the evening, Seth would take out an autoharp, rest it on his lap, and strum the few chords he could read out of a music book. Everyone else sang, even Peter. Perhaps it was due to Seth, or perhaps it was due to living with all the doughty Bakers, but Peter seemed more and more strengthened. And, to no small degree, it was also true for Jennifer. Walter's death, though it remained painful, was less devastating.

Meanwhile, outside, blizzards repeatedly swept across the unimpeded prairie. So furious could the winds be, and so blinding the snow, that Seth strung clothes lines along the deeply etched paths from the soddy to his outbuildings to help him find his way. He told stories of people who lost their way in such storms and froze to death only yards from their houses.

Of course, it was best not to challenge a blizzard to begin with but to wait it out indoors, where the thick earthen walls of the soddy did much to keep the cold out and the heat in. But on the bitterest days, the cold didn't stay politely outside—it seeped in through the door and shutters, squeezing everyone inside closer and closer to the fireplace, which wasn't nearly as efficient as a good cookstove. It was the main job of the children, each taking a turn, to keep the fire stoked. For this they used the large, platter-like buffalo chips, twists of hay, corn cobs, and the dead, woody stalks of sunflowers.

During particularly brutal blizzards, with the wind howling and the snow banked high against the walls, slowly entombing the soddy, Jennifer hugged her children close, regretting that she had ever let herself be talked into staying the winter. She wasn't frightened for herself as much as for her children, who, with their father gone, counted on her decisions for their welfare. Jennifer feared she had blundered this time. Morbid thoughts entered her head. She only hoped that, come the spring, her own and her children's bodies might be discovered by people and not wolves. No one else in the soddy knew she was thinking such things, or noticed when a tear rolled down her cheek.

But Jennifer never became totally bereft of hope. She remembered her resolve to withstand each ordeal and see it as temporary, survivable, and even strengthening. And when she was especially hard-pressed, she need only to observe Lucy Baker, who never looked worried. Even as ice began to creep under the door across the hard floor, and the frosty air penetrated farther in from the shuttered windows, tightening ever more around the huddled people, Lucy—as well as Seth—retained a calm that reassured everyone else. Jennifer marvelled at the woman's stoicism—but she also wondered how much of it was facade.

You are not fooling me entirely! thought Jennifer as she observed Lucy's performance. I know your game! And I can feign strength as well as you!

And she tried. Yet she could not quite succeed at this as well as Lucy. Much to her chagrin, Jennifer found that she was looking up more and more to her hostess. Indeed, Jennifer soon found that she wanted only to please her, like some little girl trying to please a parent. She felt a warm glow whenever she received a compliment from her. "Oh, these are such tasty corn cakes!" said Lucy one day when Jennifer was baking. Jennifer couldn't help it. She was very proud.

It was only the presence of her own children that reminded her that she herself was a grownup and ought not to be looking up to Lucy so much, or to be taking so many orders from her. It was then she thought, as she had done countless times before, "Who does she think she is?" And she kept wishing the winter would hurry and be over so she could leave—and not just the soddy but Kansas.

But the winter would not hurry. It seemed only to entrench itself more firmly upon the prairie, and Jennifer didn't think anything could ever again pry it loose. When Seth went to the chickencoop one morning, he found that some of the chickens had frozen to death upright on their roosts during the night. In the stable, he found the horses and cows had their muzzles stuck to the railing in front of them by ice blocks formed of their own vapor. Seth had to knock the ice away so that the animals could move their heads and breath freely.

The temperature had now dropped so low, and the frigid air had infiltrated into the soddy so far, that the heat from the fireplace was compacted into a small bubble. Those who faced the fire warmed only their fronts. Their rears remained chilly. This was responsible for many sniffles among the children. Lucy treated them all with hot teas and plasters, and they seemed better for it.

But Jennifer, already annoyed at herself for playing the little girl to Lucy, insisted she herself tend to Peter, who was laid up in bed. She practically had to press Lucy out of the way, but she sat near her son to take over the nursing duties. She wished she could just wrap him up, and Emma too, and run away with them lest they forget who their mother was.

But that would have to wait. The winter was still fastened to the prairie, howling across the rooftop and pounding on the shutters. All Jennifer could do—all anyone could do—was stoke the fire, huddle with the others, and pray that it didn't get colder.

For a while, it almost seemed as if the prayers worked, for the bubble of heat around the fireplace had grown. Jennifer could now step back from the hearth and feel the warmth halfway to the white-washed walls. The next morning, she was able to stand right up against the walls and still feel the warmth. At long last! The cold had been pressed back out of the soddy! The temperature outside must have been rising!

But when Jennifer, standing in the middle of the room, joyfully announced this, Seth, who was holding Mary on his knee and drawing on a slate with her, said, "I wouldn't count on that just yet, Jenny. Sorry, but the house is just banked up with snow. The snow's warmer than the air, and it protects us from the wind."

Jennifer's spirits sank. She shuffled over to a chair and plopped down into it. She was ready to go mad.

It was now three months that she was in the soddy, three months of breathing stale cold air, seeing mostly by the smoky light of lanterns and candles, forever crowded into this or that corner by children who were always under foot, and— for the benefit of her own children—all the while trying not to play the little girl. This required vigilance.

It was only at night, when she was in bed and surrounded by pitch blackness, that Jennifer felt most comfortable, for then she could at least imagine herself back in Ohio. Unfortunately, there was the occasional night when even this escape was denied her, for she would hear, not several yards from her, the discrete but clearly amorous exertions of Lucy and Seth. Jennifer sadly remembered her own, quieter lovemaking with Walter. "I love you," Lucy whispered to Seth, their blanket rustling.

The next morning, Jennifer inevitably felt her cheeks blush when she greeted her hosts, and she had trouble looking them in the eye.

And so, still more days and nights passed, and Jennifer was entertaining gloomy thoughts more and more, until one day in mid-March it was Seth himself who felt a slight change in the temperature. When he went outside to check on the animals, he noticed that the cloud of steam from his mouth was smaller and disappeared more quickly. Also, the air didn't sting his cheeks so much. When he went back into the soddy a little later, he made sure to tell all this to Jennifer.

"Thank God," she murmured.

Sure enough, with the passing of each week, then each day, the air outside—despite disheartening bouts of returning cold—was getting mostly warmer. Under the gaze of a bright yellow sun, the top layer of snow began to melt. It froze again at night, forming a smooth sheet of ice that crunched underfoot, but then it melted some more the next day. It went on like that for a week or so, freezing and melting, freezing and melting, until it kept on melting even through the night. The shoveled paths got shallower and shallower, until the gentle, mostly flat contour of the land could once again be detected beneath the smooth, white surface.

Jennifer was tantalized. She longed for the day when she could once more see the brown earth buried below. Each morning, when Seth returned from his chores, she asked him if the snow anywhere had at last melted down to the ground. Each time, however, even after spring had officially begun, he could only tell her, "Sorry, not that I could see." Sometimes, even, he reported that it had snowed again.

But on one particularly clear morning in early April, Seth went out to do his chores and didn't return for quite a while. Lucy couldn't imagine what was taking him so long and was about to send Todd out after him. But then Seth did return, a great big smile on his face. And, like the dove who returned to give Noah the olive branch, he approached Jennifer, who was sitting forlornly near the hearth, and he gave her a bouquet of fragrant, short-stemmed, lavender flowers.

Chapter Eleven
Big Bluestems

Jennifer stood beneath the Baker's leafless elm. At her feet were tracks in the snow, Seth's, that led from the soddy out into the distance where, all up and down the prairie, brown patches of sod showed through the tattered white blanket of winter. Huddled within these patches were blossoming pasqueflowers, like those Jennifer held in her hands, and white-petaled mats of flowers that Seth called cat's-foot.

"I said I would be leaving in the spring," she said, her eyes fixed on the welcomed reemerging land. "It's now spring."

"No," said Lucy, standing a few feet behind her, holding her shawl about her narrow shoulders. "You said you would wait until the railroad arrived."

Jennifer turned towards Lucy. She didn't care what she had promised. But the idea of a train whisking her home made her chest swell with anticipation. "Yes," she said, reconsidering and returning her attention to the distant flowers. "I did say that."

Jennifer stayed at the Bakers another few days while the snow melted. Then she loaded up the buggy and, with her children, left for her dugout. The snow was almost gone, leaving only some beard-like remnants along some northern sides of the rises. The once blackened land that had become white had now turned pale green as the down of new grass sprouted from horizon to horizon, punctuated here and there with those purple-and-white flower clusters. Both grass and flowers were so short that they only just quivered in the wind.

At first, Jennifer couldn't find her dugout because it was so well concealed in the down-covered slope. But she saw her water well and the burnt remains of the wagon, and then she knew where to look. Sure enough, there, in the side of the slope, were three tell-tale holes for the windows and door—but only holes?

Something was wrong. The door and window shutters were gone. Could they have blown off during a winter storm? When Jennifer rode still closer, she saw that not only were the door and shutters gone, but their very frames as well.

"Momma, what happened?" asked Emma.

"Someone broke in," said Peter, growing alarmed and trying to stand in the slowly moving buggy.

Jennifer stopped the buggy and watched the dugout from a distance. No one seemed to be on her property. She started the buggy up again and proceeded even more slowly, keeping her eyes fastened on the three dark sockets.

"Do you think Indians did it?" asked Emma.

"Wilkes!" declared Peter. "He's no good."

Jennifer pulled up before the dugout. Peter and Emma made as if to jump down. "No! Stay here!" shouted Jennifer. Then she herself descended onto the mat of new grass, and cautiously entered the rectangular opening that had once held the door.

The inside was lit only by the faint light entering from the three openings. But it was plain enough to see what was there: everything that had been left behind during the winter—the rocker, bureau, mantel clock, table and chairs, crates, even the missing door and shutters—all had been stacked up in the middle of the room and set on fire. All were in a cool, charred heap. The pungent odor of smoke still filled the dugout.

"What happened to our things?" came Emma's voice from the doorway.

"I told you to stay in the buggy!"

Peter, meanwhile, slipped past his sister and walked about the rubble. "Wilkes," he repeated dramatically.

Jennifer searched through the pile to see if there was anything salvageable, her fingers becoming blackened. The daguerrotype of her father was burnt up, as were all her books, including her little *Bridal Greetings*. Jennifer's throat tightened: as it was, Ohio had become an ever vaguer memory; now she had not even her old possessions to help her remember.

"Back into the buggy," she said, pressing her children outside and up onto the buggy seat.

"Are we going back to the Bakers?" asked Emma.

"To town!" snapped Jennifer.

Jennifer found Bill Wilkes, as usual, in Franz Hoffmann's store, Franz apparently being one of the few people who still spoke with, or at least still deigned to listen to, the land agent. Wilkes, his holster casually untied from his leg, was leaning back on a chair near the pickle barrel in the center of the room, stroking his side-whiskers, which were thicker than ever as if he had not yet shed his winter coat. He tried carrying on a conversation with the distracted merchant, who was tending a farmer couple at the counter. Several other farmers were walking about the cramped store, ignoring Wilkes, or sometimes looking askance at him, while they waited patiently for Franz and examined the various merchandise.

When Jennifer entered the store—her children left in the

buggy—Wilkes' expression at first turned sour, his eyes cold. But then he forced himself to smile at her, nod, and even tip his hat.

"Goot morning!" called Franz from his counter, noticing Jennifer's entrance.

The customers in the store also turned to offer their greeting, but Jennifer ignored them and stalked up to the land agent. He raised his eyebrows. He waited for Jennifer to speak, but all she could do for a moment was stand there and fume. "Mrs. Vandermeer?" he prompted.

"You leave me alone," she hissed.

Everyone in the room froze. Wilkes' raised eyebrows furrowed in confusion. He tilted his chair slowly forward as if this would help him understand better. "Come again?"

"You just leave me alone," repeated Jennifer, trying to keep herself from crying.

Wilkes rose to his feet to get the upper hand. He tilted his head curiously. "I'm not following."

One of the customers, Aaron Whittaker—the square-built man with short white hair—stepped toward the two. "Jenny," he said in his deep, hoarse throat, "is something the matter?"

Jennifer raised her chin as if to pretend she were braver. "I think Mr. Wilkes here knows."

"I don't think I do," said Wilkes, squinting at the slender woman.

"You like setting fires, don't you?" asked Jennifer with a forced smile.

At this, Wilkes darkened. "Now, I heard I've been blamed for that fire . . . "

"Well, add to that the one in my dugout!" said Jennifer resolutely.

"You had a fire in your dugout?" asked Aaron Whittaker.

Jennifer kept her eyes locked on the land agent. "I returned there after staying with the Bakers this winter, and I found

130

that everything there, including my door and window shutters, had been burned."

"Now, I think I'm beginning to lose my patience with these accusations," said Wilkes, returning Jennifer's stare. "Everyone knows it's Indians that set fires out here . . . "

"Oh no, sir, I won't let you blame the Indians—not for these fires . . . "

"Oh you won't, won't you," said Wilkes, trying to hold his temper. "Well, ma'am . . . " Wilkes stopped. He had by now become almost flustered. He had to start again, "Ma'am, to tell you the truth, I don't care who set them!"

"But we do," growled Aaron Whittaker, stepping closer.

Wilkes turned to face the short, stocky man. "You're awfully quick to take this lady's side."

"No," came back Aaron. "I've given it a lot of thought. We all have. Wilkes, it seems to me you've been trying real hard to get rid of us for some time now."

"You just watch what you say, Aaron," returned Wilkes. "You've got no proof . . . "

"We've got proof enough!" blurted another customer, a lanky man standing by his red-bonneted wife at the counter. The couple, along with everyone else about the room, had their attention fixed on the three by the pickle barrel.

"You like bullying ladies and children, don't you," growled Aaron, his eyes on Wilkes.

The other customers began to crowd around the two. Jennifer tried stoutly to hold her position. But she was being nudged by the people behind her, all of them edging forward and scolding Bill Wilkes over and around her shoulders.

"Look, Aaron, I'm going to let you walk way," said Wilkes, "and I'll forget all this."

"You will, will you?" asked Aaron Whittaker. "And what if I don't forget?"

"So don't forget!" erupted Wilkes, his voice cracking, his face reddening. "What are you going to do? Lynch me?"

"If there was a tree in this town . . . "

"Well, there ain't!"

"So instead you're going to make good on the property you destroyed."

"Oh no, I won't pay for something I didn't do!"

"If I have to take it out of your hide," said Aaron, stepping closer, his fists clenched.

"To hell with you!" shouted Wilkes, pushing past Aaron. But the older man spun him about. Wilkes struck out, his fist grazing Aaron's jaw. Aaron, eyes flashing, charged Wilkes, slamming him back against the wall and pinning him. Wilkes drew his gun.

"No!" shrieked Jennifer.

But even as the gun cleared the holster, the other farmers jumped its owner, several grabbing his arm and wrist. The gun was forced up as it roared, discharging into the ceiling, causing Jennifer to nearly jump out of her skin.

"Let go . . . " shouted Wilkes, his gun barrel waving over everyone's head. But the farmers dared not let go of his gun arm. Instead, they dragged Wilkes down. "Get . . . off!" he groaned. One man stepped on his wrist with a heavy workboot, and Wilkes finally released the gun, which thudded onto the floor.

Aaron snatched it away. He stood up and back, breathing heavily. "Wilkes, you just outstayed your welcome in this town," he croaked. "Someone go get his horse."

"You can't do this!" yelled Wilkes from the floor, struggling to break free of the many strong, gnarly hands pinning him. "I'm a government agent! Let . . . me . . . up!"

The farmers obliged. They lifted Wilkes up and hauled him, kicking and screaming, outside. One of the farmers returned with Wilkes's bay in tow. Following just behind the horse was Frank Turner, who stopped to watch at a distance.

"Now, don't you show your face around here again,"

growled Aaron as the rest of the farmers pushed Wilkes up atop his horse.

Wilkes, his hair mussed, his shirttail out, kicked back at them with his pointy boots. "Get away! You've no right! I own property!"

The lanky farmer slapped the horse on his rump, and off the animal trotted, nearly throwing the agent off. But Wilkes grabbed the reins and kept his seat. He stopped his horse at the north edge of town. "You'll pay for this!" he shouted. "All of you!"

Aaron Whittaker pointed the gun at Wilkes, and the land agent spun his horse around and galloped out, the report of the gun spurring him on, though Aaron had aimed it in the air.

Letting the gun rest at his side, Aaron now stepped up to Jennifer, who had taken her place by her frightened children on the buggy seat. With beads of sweat on his broad forehead, Aaron rested a thick hand on the front wheel. "Don't you fret, Jenny," he said. "We'll fix up your dugout." Then he turned to the others. "Someone get a crowbar and pick! Wilkes is about to make good!"

Two farmers ran back past Frank Turner. "Mind if we borrow some tools?" one of them called. Frank shrugged his permission. The two went into his shop and returned with the tools. Then, as Jennifer watched, her mouth agape, the farmers set to gouging out the sod walls of Wilkes's storefront—that is, removing from it his door and two windows.

"Someone give a hand here."

"Careful with the panes."

"Get the wagon."

Jennifer glanced out of town and saw the now small, distant figure of Wilkes on the prairie trail. He had stopped to look back. Jennifer was certain he was glaring back at her. Then he turned his horse and continued riding off.

"Sit down," hissed Jennifer at her children, who were all

agog. They sat. Jennifer flicked the reins. She left town, and fortunately in the opposite direction from Bill Wilkes.

By day's end, Jennifer had a new door and two new, if slightly cracked, glass-paned windows. After also rebuilding the stall, the farmers readied to leave, loading up their tools into their wagons. Jennifer stood back from her dugout and marveled at her reclaimed home. What a big difference glass windows made!

But it didn't stop there. All that afternoon and the next day, she received a steady stream of visitors, led off by Lucy Baker, all bearing gifts for their school teacher: blankets, tableware, all-purpose packing crates...

Naturally, Joseph Caulder came, too. He gave Jennifer an old, wooden chair for her dugout and seeds for a vegetable garden. The seeds Jennifer readily accepted, but, fearing Isaac's reaction to losing a chair to her, she said, "No, I couldn't take it . . . " Joseph left the chair outside her dugout and started hoeing the garden.

Several days later, Karl Pfeffer found outwhat had happened. Not to be outdone by his rival, he brought Jennifer two chickens and a cushioned parlor chair. The chickens Jennifer also readily accepted, but the parlor chair was much too nice to accept as a gift. "Really, Karl, I couldn't . . . "

But Karl dropped the chickens outside her doorstep and pressed his way inside with the chair, which he placed near the cookstove, shunting Joseph's gift aside. "Goot!" he declared, stepping back and admiring his own addition to the room.

Jennifer sighed but was grateful for all these gifts. And she was flattered that her neighbors should rally around so. Only she was beginning to have second thoughts about having accused Bill Wilkes so quickly and in front of everybody. Perhaps he was telling the truth, after all. Perhaps it had been the Indians.

134

But, really, she was most concerned that Wilkes might return with an eye towards revenge—and here she was, living in the middle of nowhere. The idea unnerved her, and she prayed that the blessed train would arrive in Four Corners to take her and her children away before anything happened.

So she settled into her newly done home, resumed her routine, even beginning to teach again, but what she did mostly was wait.

And wait.

Days turned into weeks. Outside her dugout door, she witnessed a prairie transformed continually. Those first flowers of the season were eventually joined, and replaced, by others that her children could identify, having learned the names from their school friends—flowers with such descriptive names as bird's-foot violets and Indian paintbrush. But then these flowers, in turn, were soon overwhelmed by the grasses, which all the while were growing taller and darker, so that the flowers were necessarily replaced by longer-stemmed ones, among which were those Peter and Emma called prairie violets and false indigo.

But in all that time, there came no railroad, not even word of one.

And no letter.

Jennifer had hoped she might at least receive a response from her father. Surely he had gotten her letter. Surely he meant to write back. Maybe, thought Jennifer with some amusement, his letter is on the train.

And so the weeks continued to slip by. The days grew still warmer, the grasses ever higher, and still longer-stemmed flowers blossomed, splotching the green sea with rippling rafts of crimsons, yellows, purples, and golds, until they, too, began to drown in the ever-rising tide of grasses.

And it wasn't only the grasses and flowers that were growing. The hems of Emma's dresses had risen to just below the little girl's knees. Peter's pants were above his ankles.

And neither child could fit comfortably into his or her shoes. They went barefoot. More and more, it seemed to Jennifer, Peter and Emma were looking like all the other children in the class. Peter, in fact, began to call her "Maw," what the Baker children called Lucy—a change Jennifer didn't welcome.

And still she waited. Before she knew it, spring had peaked and was already fading. The tallest flowers yet were now appearing in the swelling grasses: the daisies, larkspur, and wild roses. Then, one hot day in early July, while washing clothes in a tub before her dugout, sleeves rolled up, dark hair drawn tightly back in a bun, Jennifer noticed familiar pink flowers, mostly because of all the hoardes of monarch butterflies fluttering about them. Emma, who was helping with the wash, told her mother what they were: milkweed.

Jennifer remembered now. These were the flowers that had greeted her when she first arrived in Four Corners. But could it be? Had she really been there a year? And yet not even for such an occasion as that did the weeks pause, for it didn't seem so long before a different, and still sadder, anniversary arrived.

Jennifer and her children hadn't been to the cemetery since Walter was buried. It looked very different. The grasses had infiltrated the tombstones, except for where there were some freshly dug sites, mostly on the perimeter. Jennifer and her children waded their way from one marker to the other, brushing back the tawny-green grass. When they found Walter's grave, they bent those tough grasses back and tugged at them until they could read the stone's inscription. Then they stood silently before the marker, Jennifer embracing her children by their shoulders. She and Emma cried softly while Peter clenched his jaw and wiped away the occasional stray tear from his reddened cheek.

Still, the weeks passed. And while during that time there came no railroad—and Jennifer was beginning to think there never would be—there did arrive a letter. It was dropped off at Pearson's Inn with other mail from the east by westward-bound homesteaders. The letter, however, was not the one Jennifer expected.

> *Dear Jenny,*
> *Can anyone be as unfortunate as I? What news I have to tell you! Your letter, meant for your father's eyes, has instead reached mine. And now I sit before my desk, wondering how to tell you what I must. If only you hadn't lost Walter! My dear, poor thing, just when you need solace the most, I must compound your woes, for your father, too, has passed away . . .*

Jennifer, standing on the loose planking before the inn, stared glassy-eyed at those scribbled words of Dorothy Owens, her neigbhor back in Ohio. "Poppa? Gone?"

> *. . . Your very house has been sold to pay for his debts. What unfriendly people live there now! Oh, if only there had been someone else to tell you this . . .*

Jennifer closed her eyes tightly. A tear dribbled down her cheek. So all this time her Poppa had not been sitting before the hearth, awaiting her return. He had been in the cold ground! Like Walter! Oh, it smacked of a conspiracy! If she didn't know better, Jennifer would have sworn the two had actually arranged it that way, to sneak off together, leaving her with her earthly burdens so they could pal around in Eternity!

"Is the letter from Grandpoppa?" came Peter's voice as the boy stepped up, holding his sister's hand. Both had green-striped candy sticks from Franz's store.

Jennifer gazed at her children. "Get in the buggy," she said stiffly. "I have something to tell you."

That night, the dugout was silent. Peter kept trying not to cry, but sometimes he broke down. At one point, Emma, teary-eyed, went up to her mother rocking in her chair before the cookstove. "Is Grandpoppa keeping Poppa company?" she asked, her eyes red.

The very notion angered Jennifer. Her own eyes watery, she began rocking harder. "I imagine so," she said curtly.

Then later, with her children sleeping in their corner, Jennifer calmed down enough to come to a sobering realization—there was no longer anyone waiting for her back home. There wasn't even a house there. No Poppa. No hearth. Suddenly, she felt her feet take root in the dirt floor— as if, with no connection back home, and after now having lived in that hillside for so long, she had just at that moment become—like all the animals, grasses, and flowers around her—part of the prairie's sod.

This she could not let happen. "No, I am not a prairie plant," she murmured. "I can return east. And I will."

Autumn arrived. It was Jennifer's second autumn in Kansas, and this time around she recognized, from lands that had been spared the fire the previous year, the prairie's apparent cycle of the seasons. This was the time of the year when the grasses, having reached their greatest height, were now tawny and ready to wither, when those tallest flowers of all—the yellow goldenrod and sunflowers—were blooming, and when her students, all a year older, again departed to help their families with the harvesting.

But, this time around, there was something she hadn't before seen—at least not in such great numbers...

Chapter Twelve
The Prairie Widow

The ground was littered with grasshoppers. When she went to the well, Jennifer would knock one or two off the bucket. When she went to the stall, she'd find several clinging to the sod walls. And when she went to the garden, she found the most, all eating away at the leaves of her lettuce, potatoes, and watermelons. Karl Pfeffer's chickens chased them around with outstretched necks, trying to gobble them up, but without much success.

"Where did they all come from?" wondered Jennifer out loud as she and her children walked through the vegetables to knock away and squash the big, jointy-legged insects with the children's old shoes.

Then, while her children worked, Jennifer noticed off to the northwest a strange cloud. It was massive and stretched clear along the length of the horizon. Jennifer at first thought it was an approaching storm and worried about her dugout flooding. But it didn't really look like a storm cloud.

Then she thought it might be smoke. Another prairie fire? "Wilkes!" she gasped. But, no, it didn't look like smoke either.

This cloud scintillated, almost as if, brushing through the atmosphere, it were crackling with static electricity. Also, it seemed to move faster than the wind was blowing, as if it had a life of its own.

Below the cloud Jennifer now noticed a distant, solitary horseman, or rather muleman, riding on the trail in her direction. Jennifer hoped it was Joseph. He would know what the cloud was. But when, finally, the man had gotten close enough, Jennifer saw that it was Isaac.

"Why, Mr. Caulder!" called Jennifer from her door when Issac had at last reached earshot. "I never expect a visit from you!" She waited till he was close enough so that she could lower her voice. "I'm delighted."

Isaac Caulder didn't answer. He just kept up a steady walk on his mule until he came right up to Jennifer.

"Morning, Mr. Caulder!" called Emma, standing up a moment from her work in the garden. "Did you ever see so many grasshoppers?"

Isaac Caulder ignored the child.

"They do seem to be all over," said Jennifer, looking about her. "But come in. I can spare a moment and make us some tea."

Isaac Caulder looked grimmer than usual. His jaw was unshaven. His tired eyes were sunken, his hat slouched low. His whole body hunched over the saddle pommel as if he might soon topple. He seemed so loath to move that he hadn't even bothered to knock away a grasshopper that clung to his beaten coat and another that stubbornly clung to a long, flicking ear of his mule. "I didn't come for tea," muttered Isaac.

Jennifer lifted her chin, preparing to defend herself once more. "You seem upset over something. I do hope it doesn't involve that chair Joseph gave me. I told him . . . "

"I didn't come for the chair." Isaac ground his jaw muscles. "I've come to set something right." The grim man swallowed hard. His eyes focused on the grasshopper-spangled ground. "I come to give you and Joe my blessing."

Jennifer pressed back and placed an open hand on her chest. "Your blessing!"

"And I hope to get your forgiveness."

Jennifer softened. She shook her head sympathetically. "You needn't apologize for anything. I know I must have seemed an intruder. But why don't you come in so we can talk?"

"Ain't possible. I'd only bring more ruin on your home."

"Heavens, Mr. Caulder, you are being more puzzling today than usual."

"In the Bible it tells of a ship that nearly sunk 'cause it had a sinner aboard. God wasn't appeased until that sinner was thrown over."

"That was Jonah!" came in Emma, proudly displaying her knowledge. "He was swallowed by the whale!"

"I'm a sinner," said Isaac. "And I'm leaving before God scourges this land."

"Mr. Caulder," said Jennifer slowly, "I'm still not sure I'm following you."

But even as she spoke, Jennifer found herself distracted by that cloud, which, so much closer now, was filling the sky behind the slumped man on his mule.

"I sinned twice against you," continued Isaac, his mule pawing the ground nervously and grunting, as was the mule in the stall. "And then I sinned against Bill by letting him take the blame."

Jennifer, still distracted by the cloud, only barely heard her mumbling neighbor. "Take the blame? For what? What are you saying?" Then Jennifer fell silent. She stared up at the bedraggled man. "My God, Mr. Caulder, you don't mean it was you . . ."

"But I'm setting it straight," said Isaac. "Like I said, you and Joe got my blessing."

The cloud behind Isaac Caulder was closer. It moved in great undulating layers, like huge waves of an ethereal sea, its front portions breaking now and then upon the prairie below.

"And you don't fret about this scourge," said Isaac. "It'll follow me out."

"Mr. Caulder," said Jennifer, not sure where to direct her attention anymore, "if I understand you correctly, then we've done a great injustice to Mr. Wilkes."

"Justice will be done," assured Isaac, tugging at his reins and turning his restless mount away. "God has rooted out his sinner." He started off slowly toward the tall grass.

Jennifer wished to call out to him, but she could no longer ignore the cloud, which loomed shimmering ever nearer. It engulfed so much of the sky by now that it threatened to swallow the noon sun. And from it could be heard a low hum.

Just then, a grasshopper landed on the ground next to Jennifer. As if the ground were too hot, it jumped up with a click and landed several feet away. Then a second grasshopper landed farther off, hopped with a click and settled near her. These were followed by a third and fourth grasshopper, also hopping with clicks and resettling, and then by still others, all landing here and there, hopping with clicks, and relanding like so much popping corn. Before long, there were so many grasshoppers falling to the ground, the two excited chickens were having better luck in catching them.

Then the hum grew louder. The sun darkened. And as Jennifer glanced up, seeing the sun dimmed as if behind a scrim, the great cloud burst upon the land like a blizzard of frenzied flecks and glinting sparks, the air filled with a whirring roar. Isaac Caulder, moving off, was lost from view. Indeed, so thick was the blizzard that objects much closer—the well, the stall where the mule bayed wildly, the dugout itself—all disappeared in the blinding storm. Jennifer and her children became quickly spangled with dropping, clinging grasshoppers, which struck hard, like hail. Jennifer frantically tried brushing them off, only to have more settle upon her. "Get inside!" she finally shouted over the din as she shielded her mouth with one hand. She rushed to sweep her children, whom she could hardly see, to shelter.

"Get them off!" cried Emma, cringing frozen where she had been working in the garden and covering her face. Jennifer ushered both her and Peter toward the dugout.

The ground had quickly become inches thick with grasshoppers, and each footstep squished several of them into a slimy mash, smearing the children's bare feet. Only paces from her door, Jennifer herself slipped on the slushy bodies. As she pushed herself up, her open hand crunched even more of them. Peter darted out to help his mother, but Jennifer lifted herself and pushed him back into the dugout, whereupon she slammed the door behind her.

"Get them off!" repeated Emma, her hands swiping at her sleeves and dress, whose green hem had attracted a particularly thick congregation of grasshoppers. Her mother and brother swiped away at her dress. By the time the grasshoppers had been knocked off, the hem was gone.

Shuddering, Peter next began to shake his own shirt, for grasshoppers had dropped into it, and Jennifer began to shake out her dress. Emma helped, knocking away grasshoppers from her mother's tusseled hair and onto the dirt floor, where many insects crawled about on long, backward-jointed legs.

Meanwhile, beyond the window, the wide open prairie was no longer to be seen but only the thick roiling air. Some grasshoppers were trying to climb up the panes, only to slide back down again, their bulbous eyes staring blankly inside. Others, in whirring flight, kept thudding against the panes. One pane, which had already been cracked during the transfer from town, now broke, and grasshoppers began flitting into the dimly lit room and settling on the floor, table, chairs, and walls. A few sizzled when they landed on the stove, and a few struggled and then drowned in a pot of water.

Jennifer rushed to stuff one of her blouses into the jagged opening of the window. Meanwhile, those grasshoppers already inside were everywhere eating. They ate into a sack of flour, they pressed themselves into a sugar bowl, they blanketed a loaf of bread, they filled a basket of vegetables from the garden, and they set upon some folded linen lying on the crate. They even gnawed at the sweat-stained handle of the scythe leaning in the corner. Jennifer started for the broom, but its bristles were already being devoured. "Swat them with the books!" she ordered.

"Will they eat us, too?" cried Emma, as she timidly poked at grasshoppers feasting on a McGuffey Reader.

Jennifer knocked them off and grabbed a book. "They will not," she said, her voice trembling. "This will pass."

And the three went about the room, swatting at the all-devouring creatures with books. When they were done, the room was splotched with crushed grasshopper bodies. Most of the clothing and linen were in tatters. What did survive was stained by the insects' brown spit, which was like tobacco juice.

Meanwhile, the roar outside had stopped. The windows once more showed blue sky and open land. "Did they go?" asked Peter, still grasping a book.

Jennifer went to the window. The grasshoppers had not gone. The grass from the dugout to the horizon was scythed down and flat, buried beneath a thick mat of the seething insects. Here and there, a solitary grasshopper took off like a stray spark from the smoldering mass.

The maddened mule had run off, his tether eaten through by the grasshoppers. The hay-covered stall itself had caved in from the weight of the dropping insects. The two chickens, perhaps feeling luckier, were crazed by the manna, and, though they had already become fat and round and could not move so fast, they continued to walk atop the churning insect bodies, their scrawny necks stretched downward as they plucked up grasshopper after grasshopper.

Jennifer threw her tattered shawl about her shoulders and

stepped outside. "Momma, don't!" cried Emma. She made as if to follow, but neither she nor her brother were eager to step barefoot onto the insects.

"Close the door!" said Jennifer, turning. Her children did so to keep more grasshoppers from spilling in. Then they hurried to a window.

"Maw!" came Peter's muffled voice from behind the pane.

But Jennifer walked away from the dugout. As she did so, she stirred up grasshoppers in her path, sending them hopping and flying in sprays and splashes. It wasn't long before the lower part of her skirt was covered with the clinging insects. But she paid them little mind. She passed the garden, where all that could be seen of her vegetables were shards of watermelon rind embedded in the mat of jostling insects. She stopped by the well. Its sod wall was covered with grasshoppers. The bucket held a soup of dead and drowning insects. An acrid smell arose from both the bucket and from the well pit. And as she looked out at the unearthly vista, Jennifer saw no bird, no butterfly, but she heard something else upon the wind—the crunching of millions upon millions of tiny jaws eating, eating . . .

What madness! thought Jennifer. The sky forever buffets this land, and pounds it, and spits on it, and tears at it!

And yet, even as she gazed upon a prairie once more besieged, she knew that the sod below was already pregnant with the grasses and flowers that would emerge next spring. Then, as happened the year before, and would no doubt happen every year, there would return a fresh sea of grass—bluestems mostly, but others, too—and there would be all those hosts of recurring, stubborn flowers: the mats of cat's paw and pasque flower, the many asters and daisies, the aptly named bird's-foot, the milkweed with its swarms of monarch butterflies, the goldenrod, the great sunflower, and perhaps even—so it seemed—the prairie widow.